Praise for *Bottom of the Pyramid*

"Nia endured a childhood that was commodified for our mass entertainment, while having her own inner world, health, and humanity silenced. *Bottom of the Pyramid* honors the grit it took to survive such a uniquely intense experience and her commitment to challenging and revising the narratives assigned to her. There is nothing more powerful than hearing this story directly from the source—in Nia's own words."

—Alyson Stoner

Actor, author, and founder/CEO of Movement Genius

"Nia tells her story with bravery and maturity beyond her years. She does not shy away from addressing the more difficult and complex emotions around race, identity, and growing up in the public eye. She is genuine in her explorations and in the retelling of what we might think we know from watching *Dance Moms*. It is remarkable that she emerged as a whole and well-adjusted woman from the clutches of the competitive dance world and reality TV. This is a book that reckons with the tension between having your story controlled, edited, and distributed without your direct input and telling it yourself. It is a must-read for anyone seeking deeper understanding of the fact that what you see is not necessarily the full truth."

—Danielle Prescod

Author of *Token Black Girl* and *The Rules of Fortune*

"I was hooked on *Bottom of the Pyramid* the moment I opened it—I finished in one sitting! A beautiful reminder to cherish what matters and face difficulties with courage."

—Chloé Lukasiak

Actress, author, and dancer

"Nia's memoir is a powerful testament to resilience and grace. Growing up in front of the world to witness and critique, she has emerged as a woman of great integrity who knows herself deeply. Her story will undoubtedly inspire young people to pursue their dreams while staying true to who they are."

—Alicia Graf Mack

Artistic director of Alvin Ailey American Dance Theater

"Nia Sioux's story is one of perseverance, strength, and inner peace. Anyone seeking inspiration to reach their highest potential and productivity will likely find valuable lessons in her journey. I highly recommend this motivational memoir."

—Gloria Gaynor

Global superstar and legendary singer of "I Will Survive"

"Nia leads with so much grace and strength. Her story is a beautiful reminder that you don't have to fit into someone else's mold to find your voice and make an impact. I'm so inspired by her journey and all the light she's putting into the world."

—Misty Copeland

Ballerina, author, and philanthropist

"Nia Sioux's memoir is a powerful reclamation of identity, truth, and resilience. As someone who's spent a lifetime in the dance world, I've witnessed how much courage it takes to stand tall in an industry that often tries to shrink you. Nia's story is raw, inspiring, and deeply human. She offers an unfiltered look at the price of fame, the weight of being the only one who looks like you in the room, and the strength it takes to keep showing up with grace. This book is not just about dance—it's about reclaiming your power, finding your voice, and writing your own story. I'm so proud of Nia for turning pain into purpose. *Bottom of the Pyramid* is a must-read for anyone who's ever been underestimated and dared to rise anyway."

—Cheryl Burke

Twenty-six-season *Dancing with the Stars* alumna,
mental health advocate, beauty creator, podcaster, and author

"What Nia has done in these pages is brave and beautiful. Her story is proof that you can overcome challenges and come out the other side with grace, clarity, and a deep sense of purpose. I know this book will resonate with anyone who has ever felt misunderstood, overlooked, or silenced."

—Tay Lautner

Podcast host, mental health advocate, and digital content creator

"What Nia has done here is timely and moving. She's removed the gloss on fame and perfection and delivered something so raw, so honest, and so necessary. I wish every young girl, especially young Black girls, could read this story of knowing your worth, protecting your peace, and rewriting the narrative in your own voice."

—Gabrielle Union
Actress, producer, activist, and *New York Times* bestselling author

"Nia's story is powerful and important; what she shares in *Bottom of the Pyramid* will resonate with anyone who has ever felt unseen. She leads with grace and strength, and I love the woman she's become."

—Maria Menounos
New York Times bestselling author and host of *Heal Squad* podcast

BOTTOM OF THE PYRAMID

A Memoir of Persevering, Dancing for Myself, and Starring in My Own Life

Nia Sioux

HARPER HORIZON

For my incredible mom. Forever living on the dance floor with you.

Bottom of the Pyramid

Published by Harper Horizon, an imprint of HarperCollins Focus LLC, 501 Nelson Place, Nashville, TN 37214, USA.

ISBN 978-1-4002-5305-0 (ePub)
ISBN 978-1-4002-5304-3 (HC)

HarperCollins Publishers, Macken House, 39/40 Mayor Street Upper, Dublin 1, D01 C9W8, Ireland (https://www.harpercollins.com)

Library of Congress Cataloging-in-Publication Data

Library of Congress Cataloging-in-Publication application has been submitted.

Art direction: Belinda Bass
Interior design: Kristy Edwards

Printed in the United States of America

25 26 27 28 29 LBC 12 11 10 9 8

Contents

Foreword

They say sometimes your family isn't the one you're born into but rather the one you make for yourself. It's safe to say that the original cast (and crew) of *Dance Moms* was like one big—albeit highly dysfunctional—family. For four long years, all we knew was each other. But the moment couldn't last forever, so one by one the original cast slowly withdrew until the remaining picture was mostly unrecognizable. Save, of course, for Nia.

I always admired the fact that she stayed until the very end of the show. She wanted to finish what we had started, and if any one of us was going to outlast the chaos of a reality show, I knew it would be her. For the first few years after we all began to go our own ways, we mostly avoided each other. Speaking for myself, I needed space to heal and process everything that I had gone through.

But eventually we began to find our way back to each other. Nia and I would end up in the same city at the same time and decide to quickly catch up or meet for dinner. Sometimes it was hard—just being together could jog memories of our most challenging days. But time soothed our wounds, as it often does, and we were left with an unbreakable connection. Nia is truly one of my dearest friends, and we understand each other in a way that is rare. There's a sisterhood between all of us girls. We can go an entire year without speaking to or seeing each other, but the moment we're together again, time stands still.

Just as we took time to return to each other, we all needed time to figure out how we wanted to tell our stories. Some of us choose to share frequently; others choose not to share at all. While we were there with each other, living the same days, we each had our own experiences.

When I learned that Nia had decided not to do the reunion in 2024, I was rather surprised. But when she explained that she wanted to share her past in her own time, in her own way, I understood. I'll never fully appreciate her personal experience on the show and vice versa. But this book, *Bottom of the Pyramid*, is her opportunity to reclaim her story. To retell the past in her own truth and show you all that she is who she is today through choices, not happenstance.

I'll admit that reading this book was difficult at times. It reminded me of things I had long since buried or forgotten entirely. My heart broke again for the younger versions of us who endured so much. But as Nia reminds us through her story, our hardships empower us to rise. We cannot always control our circumstances, but we can control our grit. We can face each day with grace and strength, just as she demonstrates. If you were my own blood, I couldn't be prouder of you, Nia.

Chloé Lukasiak

Introduction: Bottom of the Pyramid

When the producers of *Dance Moms* contacted me about participating in a reunion show during the spring of 2023, my immediate answer was no.

I didn't even have to think about it.

If I was going to share anything about my time on the show, it would be on my terms and my terms only.

I had already started working on a book, and though I considered that the reunion could have been a great way to announce and promote my memoir, just the thought of being among many of my former castmates made me sick with anxiety. I didn't trust them or some of the producers. Production had seven years to turn my narrative around and failed to do so. This was my time to put my foot down and show them they didn't own or control me.

When I first finished filming *Dance Moms*, I wanted to write about my experience on the show. A few of the girls had already published books, so I felt the need to share my side of the story. I'm so happy I ended up waiting. I was young and angry, and I know I would've said things I'd regret. Time away from the show allowed me to reflect and gather my thoughts. But the desire to share my story never wavered, and after a few years, I began to wonder whether it was finally the right time.

I had just started meeting with my book agent about figuring out the process when one of my closest friends, former *Dance Moms* costar Chloé Lukasiak, and I got together to hang out. We started talking about our time on the show, and Chloé expressed surprise that I hadn't yet shared my experience more outwardly. I told her I'd been scared of Abby for the longest time and was also afraid of the backlash I might receive from former castmates and the network. "You should talk about it," Chloé said confidently. "People will want to hear from you."

She floated the idea of sharing a video on YouTube to address everything, but I always knew my story needed more space to be told. It had to be a book. A year and a half later, I shared with Chloé that, while I wasn't doing the reunion show, I was writing my story. She was so excited for me, and I never regretted my decision not to attend. If anything, hearing some of the negative comments after the episode aired justified my concerns about participating. Moreover, I didn't want to allow others to railroad my story into the direction they saw fit. Everything was aligning, and I knew now was the time for my voice, my perspective, to take center stage.

When I told my parents I was ready to write my book, the first question they asked was what the title would be.

"*Bottom of the Pyramid*," I said. They understood how deep that title was for me, which was exactly why my dad worried about it. He knew I had put so much work into getting people to see me as *not* always being at the bottom. But to me, the title wasn't something negative; I was reclaiming it and turning it into a positive. After all, it's a testament to a large portion of my life.

From the age of three until well into my teenage years, I was a member of the Abby Lee Dance Company (ALDC) in Pittsburgh, Pennsylvania. Many assume I joined the studio for the show, but I was there for many years prior to the studio landing a TV deal with Lifetime in 2011. The ensuing hit *Dance Moms* would go on to air in more than 130 countries and be translated into ten different languages. The breadth and depth of the show's success was unimaginable. What started as a six-week run and then seven added episodes over the summer became a pop culture phenomenon overnight, and we girls were suddenly household names.

I remember the first time we all saw ourselves on a big screen at our premiere party in Las Vegas. It was simultaneously exciting and weird, and it never got old. Nor did the opportunities that followed, like winning a Kids' Choice Award or performing on *The View* or being nominated for several Teen Choice Awards. Each time felt refreshing and different, and we were grateful for our incredible fandom, which has, overall, proven to be supportive and loving. However, there are some who can be cruel and hurtful. It was hard reading comments that I should not have been on the team and that I was a bad dancer. Sometimes people would even quote Abby's negativity, taking her awful words as gospel. Luckily, over time, I found mentors and a dance support system who saw value in my talents. They believed in me and lifted me up despite the negativity that brewed online.

Viewers' perception of me stemmed from me always being on the bottom of "the pyramid." This pyramid was a tiered system that showed how my castmates and I ranked each week in the eyes of the founder, Abby Lee Miller, based on our dance capabilities. She would literally arrange our headshots into a pyramid shape on the mirrors in the dance studio, covering up the images so she could reveal them one by one, bottom to top, while she criticized or praised how we had performed that week. Being at the top of the pyramid was the goal. It meant you'd done something good and had her favor.

The bottom was the last place anyone wanted to be. If you were on the bottom, you'd messed up, underperformed, or otherwise found yourself out of her good graces. And the bottom was where I found myself, week after week, season after season, no matter how hard I worked.

I did not want to be known as the bad dancer. My mom and I were particularly sensitive to this because people sometimes unfairly and incorrectly assume standards get lowered for Black people. I knew I had to get better to prove that I was more than the image that had been painted of me.

After years of being the underdog—constantly told I was a terrible dancer or that I wouldn't amount to anything or that I was stupid or ugly—I often wonder how I came out whole, especially because, for the majority of my time on the show, I was the only Black girl. People tried to break me, but I never let them win. If it wasn't for my determination and the support of my amazing family, I don't know how I would have made it through.

Sadly, my story is not that uncommon. There are a lot of Black women who have been told they could not do something and that they should settle or forget their dreams. In my case, I feel like I was set up to fail. I was given choreography that was too juvenile for my age group and ability level. The songs I danced to and the costumes I wore were sometimes overtly racist, immature, or inappropriate. I was pitted against the few Black dancers who joined the team and criticized for my skin tone, the curves of my body, and even the natural hair that grew out of my scalp.

I know fans wonder why I stayed on the show for so long. The short of it is that I would not concede to anyone's opinion of me. The fact that I knew I wasn't wanted on the team only made me push harder. I needed to prove I was—*am*—good enough. That I would stick to my commitments and come out stronger, no matter what.

I was treated as if I had less to offer, but I knew myself. I was a performer. Even if the playing field wasn't level, I wasn't going to stop.

Watch me, I'd think. *I'm not going anywhere.*

Abby made it seem as if being at the bottom was the absolute worst position, and some of my castmates leaned into that notion and treated me poorly because of it. But, years later, I've come to think of this differently. Consider a cheerleading squad. When they form a pyramid, what does the bottom look like? The bottom has all the strongest members of the squad, who are there to ensure the team members do not fall. Without the bottom of the pyramid, there would be no one at the top. The pyramid wouldn't even exist. I know now that I was the glue to the team, using my strength to hold everyone together, even when no one could see it.

I've also always known one important reality: When you're at the bottom, the only place you can go is up.

Being at the bottom of the pyramid is the beginning of my story, but it most certainly is not the end. Despite barriers and constant naysayers, assumptions and criticisms, I've found within me the power to create my own narrative. I have developed a tough skin and the stamina to prove others wrong and myself right. Some may criticize me for what I have to say, or even for speaking up at all. But I've come to a place where I don't let the negativity of people I don't respect bother me. I simply don't listen to the voices of those who have harmed me. Because of where my story began, my foundation is strong, and I am grounded in resilience. Because of where my story began, I can offer it up as encouragement to others.

I'm not interested in participating in the Oppression Olympics or competing with others over who had the most difficult time on *Dance Moms*. My story is one of hardships, yes, but it's also one of strength, perseverance, triumph, and defining success for myself. The little girl at the bottom of the pyramid grew up into a young woman, and though the journey there was challenging, I hope you will find it to be equally inspiring.

Finally, I am ready to be the star in my own life.

It Takes a Village

Prior to *Dance Moms*, I had a pretty typical childhood. I lived with my parents and brothers in Churchill, the kind of cute, small Pittsburgh suburb where kids played in the street and people waved as they passed by jogging or walking their dogs. Our next-door neighbors were the best. We would have campfires and make s'mores in their backyard or play together with our dogs and take them on walks. We'd ride bikes, go to the local swimming pool, play house, and hang out in our hot tub. Whenever we were out of town, they would collect our mail and check on the house.

Some of my fondest memories are from summer vacations with my family. On Myrtle Beach, where my parents had a time-share, we spent hours walking along the shore, the sun shining bright on our skin and sand between our toes, while my mom made sloppy joes or tacos in the property's small kitchen, located just off the living room and two bedrooms. Our mornings were spent at the pool or the lazy river, while afternoons at the beach included sandcastle building and shell collecting. Sometimes we'd go mini golfing or to Medieval Times, and on rainy days we'd sit inside and play board games or watch TV shows like *Drake & Josh* or *SpongeBob SquarePants*. Taking that trip was something we looked forward to each year. It was a time when everyone was happy and carefree, our only focus on enjoying our family.

My mom and dad, Holly and Evan Frazier, always treated me like a princess. Maybe because I am the only girl of my parents' three children, sandwiched between Evan Jr. (EJ), who is two years older than me, and William (Will), who is two years my junior.

My little brother, Will, and I were the closest growing up. Best friends really, and similar in many ways. When we were kids, people often mistook us for twins, and you'd never find one of us without the other. We baked together, made pillow forts in the living room, played outside with the neighbors, and shared movie nights. Sometimes I would teach him tumbling in our living room, which got super dangerous in the small space.

EJ, on the other hand, was typically off doing his own thing or playing sports. I've always looked up to him, though, because he's such a cool guy—charming with a genuine heart. While I was a bit of a wallflower, he was the popular kid at school, and I was in constant awe of his ability to draw people in and make everyone smile. He has the best sense of humor. I like to think some of that rubbed off on me too.

Our tightknit family valued customs like eating meals together in our cozy living room, helping my mom cook in the kitchen, walking our dogs, and playing board games—especially chess. The support we've always shown one another has strongly influenced the person I am today.

In the early years of my life, my mother was the principal of our elementary and middle school, and my father was the CEO and executive director of a nonprofit social services agency called the Hill House Association. He worked closely with the residents of the Hill District in Pittsburgh to ensure they received resources vital to the community—including childcare, after-school care, dental care, health services, economic development, continuing education, and job-seeking assistance. One of his big initiatives was getting the Hill District a local grocery store. Part of the reason why I have a heart for philanthropy and want to give back in any way I can is because of my father's dedication to community service. Eventually, my dad would go on to start his own nonprofit focused on helping Black people get executive-level leadership roles. He noticed there was a big financial gap when it came to people of color in high-paying jobs and decided to do something about it. I hope to one day start a nonprofit of my own, just like he did.

With both my parents in demanding jobs, it took a village to raise us. Although my mom's parents, Gwen and William Hatcher, still lived in New York, where they'd raised my mom, they stepped in to help with tasks like babysitting, taking us to doctors' appointments, and cooking our meals. They were there whenever our family needed them. They even provided financial assistance whenever they could, like helping out with the cost of dance or buying my brothers' team uniforms. They attended any sporting events or dance competitions we were a part of whenever they could.

Some summers when I stayed with them in the city, Grandpa Hatcher would drive me to dance intensives there. One summer I attended the Dance Theater of Harlem's dance intensive, and we fell into a morning routine: He'd cook me breakfast, and we'd leave later than planned. But Grandad would drive fast, switch lanes, and honk his horn in typical New York fashion, and somehow he always got me there on time.

Likewise, my father's parents, Brenda and Andrew Frazier, helped shuttle my brothers and me to various extracurriculars. My parents introduced us to a plethora of activities at a young age. Sports, karate, art, piano lessons, swimming, drum lessons, cheerleading—you name it, we tried it. The variety of opportunities we were exposed to allowed us to decide for ourselves where our individual interests lay. My mom first put me in dance classes because she had danced recreationally when she was a child and thought dance was a fun activity for little girls. She had been taught by Vickie Sheer, a revered dance teacher who served the dance community for more than seventy-five years before her death in 2019, and whose dance competitions I would later compete in with the ALDC.

So I wasn't the first dancer in my family—and for that matter, neither was my mom, who not only was trained by Vickie Sheer but also took African dance in college. When my grandad started taking me to dance, he told me all about his brother, Henry Belcher, who was in his nineties and still tap-danced professionally. He was a part of a group called the Dancin' Demons, and they had performed on all sorts of stages, including at the famed Apollo Theater. The family connection made my love of dance even more exciting for Grandpa Frazier. He picked me up from school and dropped me off at dance for years, until he literally couldn't drive anymore.

Grandad Frazier was sweet, funny, and laid-back, while Grandma Frazier, although loving, was sterner. I guess she had to be since she was active in the civil rights movement. She did a lot of advocacy work and protested against the KKK in Pittsburgh. She was the first Black president of the Pittsburgh East End chapter of NOW (National Organization of Women) and even maintained a position in the county council. Earlier in life, she'd had a host of jobs in real estate and education.

Coming from a family of strong Black women, I see where I get my tenacity. My grandma on my mom's side, whom we call Nana, is a retired lawyer and equally brilliant. I can count on her for great advice about anything. She always knows what to say, especially when things get hard. Working in the Bronx DA's office gave her a plethora of wild stories that she uses to share life lessons.

Although not a grandparent, my aunt Heather, my mom's sister, played a vital role in my upbringing as well. She is extremely smart and accomplished—she is also a lawyer, like Nana—and is a huge adventurer who helped instill my love of travel.

It is not lost on me how blessed my siblings and I are to have known and grown up with our maternal and paternal grandparents. We are a family tied together not only by blood but by love. I'm forever thankful for their presence in my life and all the care they gave, especially when things got tough.

Since my dad often hosted community events, my family saw early on how much I loved the stage. I was always drawn to it, and though shy, I'm a bit of a drama queen. Anytime my dad was called onstage to give a speech or toast, or to introduce himself, I was right there by his side. As soon as the mic touched his fingers and he started speaking, I was reaching out to take it into my own hands. Even then I knew I wanted to be a performer.

My first dance studio was far from our house, but it was our only option because it was the only one we knew of that accepted two-year-olds. Once a week for a year, my mom would drive about an hour away to Indianola, Pennsylvania, where I would attend classes. After that year, she knew she couldn't sustain the commute; working, picking up my brothers and me from school, and then rushing to get me to dance on time was just too much. So she had to find a place closer to home. She was surprised to learn that there was a dance studio right up the street from us, Reign Dance Productions, that offered classes to students my age. This was a perfect solution! A dance studio that I could attend in my neighborhood. The decision was based solely on convenience and not on any desire for prestige or a professional career in dance.

My parents soon learned, however, that the establishment was co-owned by Maryen Lorrain Miller and her daughter, Abby Lee Miller, and Abby had credentials. Her students had gone to Broadway and danced for Disney, and she was well known in the Pittsburgh dance community. She was also certified by Dance Masters of America and was a member of Dance Masters of Pennsylvania.

You wouldn't have known any of this from driving past the studio. Although close to our home, Reign Dance Productions was literally in the middle of nowhere. Just beyond the front door was a grandiose, semicircular gray wooden structure of a desk that took up most of the space in the entryway, and to the right of it, a collage of photos of working dancers set the tone for the rest of the space. The studio was generously sized and consisted of three rooms. The upstairs viewing area overlooked all the dance rooms and offered parents a place to sit and watch their children practice. Studio A, the largest room, was the nicest, boasting Marley flooring atop a raised platform, which helped take some of the pressure off dancers' legs and feet. Most of our classes were held in this room. Studio B was, essentially, an overflow room. Though it was smaller than Studio A, it also had Marley flooring. When it wasn't being used by the younger kids for classes, the older kids would use it for more concentrated classes, like ballet. At one point we even had silk aerial classes in there. Studio C, the smallest room, had hardwood floors that weren't good for much of anything besides tap.

There was a den in the studio as well, which had a weird smell and often housed pests like ants and stink bugs. Even though the den was kind of crusty, we all loved it. It was our hangout spot, a comfortable room for us dancers to talk, stretch, do homework, eat dinner and snacks, and do our hair. Looking back, I can see how bad some of the conditions in the studio were, but it was just normal to me. This was my dance home, and I aspired to join that wall of working dancers someday.

The school had two dance tracks: recreational and competition. Recreational dancers would perform with their classes in just one recital at the end of the dance year; there were no solos, no duets, no trios, and classes were held only one day a week. Competition dancers, on the other hand, while also often performing in groups, could have a solo if Abby allowed it. The dance year ran almost the same schedule as the school year, starting in the fall and ending in June.

Recreational dance was a hobby. But to be a competition, or "company," dancer—that was serious business. Initially, my mom signed me up for recreational dance since she was familiar with it and it came with fewer obligations. But I really wanted a solo, so I had to become part of the company. Company dancers received better classes, better costumes, better choreography, and more attention from the teachers at the studio. If you were chosen as a soloist, you also received affirmation that you had talent. Being a part of the competition team represented the epitome of an elite dance experience.

Often, I would watch the older girls in the company, and I

looked up to them. They were beautiful dancers, and I was mesmerized by their routines. One dancer in particular who caught my attention was Brooke Hyland, who would also become a cast member on *Dance Moms*. Her solos were something to behold, and she seemingly won every title at every competition. Back then, my biggest goal was to do the same—to get a crown. If I did that, I'd be the winner for an entire year, just like a reigning beauty pageant queen. But to get my crown, I had to be the best, which meant a lot of practice.

From my earliest memory I was always frightened of Abby Lee Miller. Imagine being a little kid and walking into the studio. Abby is sitting at the front desk, filling the space with her tremendous presence. She is not what most people would envision when they think of a dance teacher. In fact, you've rarely ever seen Abby dance—just choreograph and teach. She is loud, big, and usually draped in black. She is intimidating, scary, and likes to yell. You'd hope Abby wouldn't be there, especially if you were late. Then she would tell you to not even bother going into class. If she is there, you quickly try to go to the den without being noticed, because you know that being noticed is an opportunity for her to find fault in you. If you wear an extra layer of clothing, she will yell at you; if you wear socks, she will yell at you. If you have a hair tie on your wrist, she will yell at you. You quickly learn that you do not want to be on her bad side.

I wasn't the only girl who was scared of Abby. We dancers would commiserate about our mutual fear. We would keep an ear out for her voice, and if we heard her coming, we'd scurry into another room before she found us. She was like a real live Miss Trunchbull from *Matilda*. Even today, the thought of her voice still sometimes freezes me in my tracks. Rather than send us flying out the door, however, her being hard on us had the opposite effect of bringing us together. We saw her harshness as a form of tough love and became a tight-knit group because of it.

Abby's focus was acrobatics, technique, and flexibility, so she tended to work a lot with the older girls. When I started as a recreational student, Mrs. Miller taught most of my classes: tap, ballet, and acrobatics. Each class was between thirty minutes to an hour. Abby's mother was so nice and had a style of teaching that was entirely different from Abby's. She was kind, gentle, and patient, even if we didn't get the moves right. Although I didn't work with Abby as much in the beginning, I knew she was always watching.

By the time I turned six, I convinced my mom to let me join the competition team. All we had to do was pay the dues and I was in, determined from the outset to earn that coveted solo. It would be difficult, but I'd seen Abby grant other six- and seven-year-olds the honor. Besides, growing up with two brothers had given me a healthy dose of competitiveness. I wasn't afraid of a challenge. This was my time to shine.

Competitive Edge

Before I joined the competition team, I attended dance class only on Wednesdays. But now that I was a part of the team, practice was after school three days a week: Monday, Tuesday, and Thursday. "Being a part of this team will take over your life," Abby warned us, but my mom didn't really understand how that could happen until it did.

On the days I had dance, I'd sit through class impatiently, waiting for school to be over so Granddad could pick me up and take me to practice. I looked forward to our routine of riding in his big sedan that smelled of cigarettes. First, we'd stop at the McDonald's by the studio to grab my favorite afternoon snack—a cheeseburger Happy Meal with ketchup only, fries, and a Sprite—and then head to dance. Practice started around four o'clock and lasted until about eight. My mom would try to make it there whenever she got off early so she could watch me dance for a little while. My brothers hated when she stayed because that meant they'd be forced to sit with her until I was done. On later nights, my dad would pick me up, often just coming home from one event or another downtown. Mom liked to joke that every night was either a chicken dinner or a reception.

Soon after I joined the competition team, the dance school was renamed the Abby Lee Dance Company. Training was a fundamental aspect of life at the ALDC—and I do mean *life at* the studio, because it felt like we lived there. I took classes in ballet, tap, and acro, plus technique-focused classes, like jumps and turns, legs and feet, and warm-up. We also had classes just for combos. In the combination classes, we'd learn a minute or so of choreography in various styles—like jazz, contemporary, musical theater, or lyrical—and then break into groups and perform that section. The combination classes were just for fun—a helpful way for us to improve our movements and pick up choreography quickly.

The competition team was broken up into age groups: minis, juniors, teens, and seniors. There were about fifteen or so of us girls in my line. To learn choreography for the competition dances, we were required to attend rehearsals outside of our regularly scheduled classes, usually on Saturdays and sometimes Sundays. Each dance had only two to three of these bonus rehearsals, so it was important that you showed up. If you didn't, you'd fall behind. This same rule applied to our individual sessions for solos. One-on-one sessions we had with a teacher were called "privates." You could purchase these sessions to work on anything you needed to: flexibility, turns, tap, or even solo practice.

Back then, in 2008, our rehearsals were never recorded, mostly due to a lack of handheld gadgets with which to film them. So I brought along a notebook and wrote down the steps we learned to help me remember them. For solo rehearsals, sometimes my mom would take notes for me, and I'd always have a good laugh when I went back to read them. She didn't know how to spell half the moves since they were either ballet terms based in French or made-up names. Thankfully, my signature step, the Jackknife, wasn't difficult to spell. I'm pretty sure the name was made up, but the move was basically a straddle jump into the air, and I was really good at it. Abby incorporated it into nearly all my routines, so Mom was always writing that move in her notes. Abby had a plethora of wild names for other moves, too, though some we didn't like to say or write. Like the floor pose that was similar to pigeon pose in yoga, which she called the "swastika pose." Mom and I never laughed about that one. I was so little I didn't understand what that word even meant. Once I learned the context, I was horrified.

During practice, we'd perfect our group routine until we were ready to compete in the four or five major dance conventions and competitions that took place every year. After a few short months to learn the solos, trios, group dances, and other routines, we would hit the competition circuit sometime after Christmas break. But our training was year-round. In the summers, we were required to take "booty camp," a one- to two-week course at the studio. The name of this session made us giggle because we wore "booty shorts" to dance class, so we thought the play on words was clever and funny. But there was nothing funny about booty camp. It was like an intense summer camp for dancers, where different choreographers would come in and teach us various techniques, tricks, combinations, and routines. I loved every second of it. Abby loved the money it made her and wasn't shy about saying so. These classes were open to the public and created a way to bring in outside money to the dance school.

Speaking of money, competitive dance is *expensive*. The cost of costumes, practices, privates, dance clothes and shoes, competitions, and travel adds up quickly and is taken on by the dancers' families. There were also team jackets, sweat suits, T-shirts, and other accessories that us company dancers had to buy—items Abby said she would often get for a discount in New York and charge us double to purchase.

As if all that wasn't enough, there was our annual dance yearbook—one of Abby's biggest moneymakers.

Picture day for the yearbook was a big event. Abby would give us an elaborate schedule where we'd rotate in and out, changing into multiple costumes, in full hair and makeup. We'd pose however she wanted us to, and the resulting photos were featured in the yearbook. If you were a part of the company, your family had to purchase a full-page ad, and you were required to buy the book as part of your fee. Abby claimed these books would be sent out to Broadway scouts and Hollywood execs; she also sold them at astronomical prices at the dance school. She told us this exposure was what helped her garner a cache of professional dancers.

However, there was one true gift that she gave us girls each year. As a Christmas present, she would buy us matching bra and panty sets because "every little girl should have underwear that matches." The younger girls, like me, got a training bra with matching panties. I didn't care that much about my own bra and underwear matching, but I did think it was cool that us girls matched one another. In my mind it made us more like sisters.

Our dance sisterhood was one of the biggest appeals of the studio. Though I'd always liked school, I didn't have many friends. So, despite the hard work, I looked forward to catching up with my dance mates and giggling about silly stuff, like who had the cutest new leotard or who could remember the combo we'd learned in the previous class. In the dance world, things were different. *I* was different. I fit in, and I finally had something in common with girls my age.

One of my closest friends was Chloé Lukasiak, who also lived in the same neighborhood as me. This was lucky since it meant her parents were often available to drop me off at home. Having three kids meant my parents were juggling a lot, carting me around to dance and karate and my brothers to flag football, karate, soccer, and lacrosse. Sometimes this meant I was the last dancer waiting to get picked up after practice. Sometimes it meant relying on Chloé's parents. I was grateful for her friendship and their help.

I was a fairly quiet and reserved kid outside of performing. I *hated* attention being drawn to me; it made me feel awkward and self-conscious—unless I was onstage. When I danced, I showed everyone how outgoing I could be. Just as Beyoncé has her alter ego, Sasha Fierce, when I went onstage, I would light up and become a whole new person.

This was also true for my performances in the studio. I would feel so nervous during rehearsal, which sometimes caused my dance teachers to get frustrated with me because they knew I was a firecracker. I liked saving my high-energy performance for the stage, but they wanted to see it from me all the time. That was a note I consistently received when rehearsing: "Come on, Nia, we need more!" I tried—I really did—but this transformation only ever seemed to kick in once the lights dimmed and I could hear the crowd, feel their energy. In those moments, I knew that I was exactly where I belonged.

After a year of being on the competition team, one night at practice, I got the best news of my life: "Nia, you'll be doing a solo." Abby said it so nonchalantly, but I was stoked. I'd been asking for one for a while, and my time had finally come.

My private session was set, and I couldn't wait to hear what song had been chosen for me. Other girls were getting popular, recognizable songs that were cute and age appropriate, so I was sure I would love mine. But it turned out to be a song I'd never heard of before. The selection was called "Nattie of the Jungle" by Ken Lonnquist, and it's about a child who is left in the wild to be raised by monkeys. The lyrics detail a girl who is unwashed, with a dirty, Tarzan-like appearance. She doesn't know how to eat from a fork and throws her banana peels on the ground. The song goes on to liken her to a gorilla before closing with the chorus and a slew of monkey sounds.

When Abby began teaching me the steps, I was genuinely excited. *Tarzan* had just come out a few years earlier, so I thought of this as my *Tarzan* dance. I loved Disney, loved animals, and thought the choppy, animal-like movements and gimmicky gestures were fun.

My mom did not. That night at rehearsal, I could see how upset she was, the emotions playing across her face. I couldn't understand why. When we got home, she shared her concerns about the song choice and choreography with my father. She worried about the "racial undertone" of it all.

Racial undertone? I wasn't entirely sure what that meant. To me, the song wasn't really a big deal. "The lyrics are funny," I explained. Even the monkey sounds in the background made people giggle. I was more bothered by Mom's reaction than the song. This was my opportunity to show that I had what it took to be like the other girls. That I could represent the ALDC. Why couldn't she see that?

Unwilling to break my heart, my parents agreed to let me do the dance. I was happy with their choice because I didn't want to rock the boat. Success at the studio was a delicate balance, and staying in Abby's good graces made things easier.

With that first competition year behind me, I couldn't wait to find out what my second solo would be.

Now eight years old, I was given another opportunity. This solo routine was choreographed by Abby to a song called "Satan's Li'l Lamb" by Sam Harris. When my mom heard the song title, she immediately voiced her concerns to Abby. She'd bitten her tongue about the "Nattie of the Jungle" routine, but she couldn't do so with this one. My family was not super religious, but we were Christians who believed in God and we often went to church on Sundays, so this song did not sit well with my parents. They worried that the context of the song would go against our religious values.

Abby reassured my mom that the song was not satanic. My costume was really cute—a white-pants-and-crop-top matching set, with rows of tassels that added flair to my movements—and the choreography was age appropriate. Once again, my parents decided to let me perform because I was so happy to have another solo. They still weren't 100 percent okay with the routine, though, and they began to question whether I should stay at the studio. I was determined not to leave the studio nor my friends, but we all agreed to discuss the possibility more when the dance year concluded.

Overall, the routine went well, showcasing my flexibility and acrobatic talents. I had finally gotten Abby's attention, and I was on cloud nine. The first time she seemed to have taken notice of me was when she gave me a special part in a dance called "My Hair Looks Fierce." It was a jazz dance, and although I wore an afro wig, it was quite fitting for the dance since everyone wore a wig. One dancer had a mohawk, another had big fluffy hair—the routine was fun and funky. I exuded stage presence and attitude, which is what I think drew Abby to me. My energy shined through in our group dances, which is why I started being given special spotlight moments in our routines. Whether at the beginning of the dance or at the end, I would make a statement, giving face and lots of attitude.

One year we did a group dance called "Chicks," in which we dressed up like little chicks with feathers on our heads. I started out the dance by hopping in a squatted position, my arms mimicking tiny wings. Then I ended the dance by yelling a big "BAWK!" on the stage. Everyone thought it was so cute, and all the students at the dance studio loved me in it.

There are some things that can't be taught, and for me that spark was innate. Getting those spotlight roles made me feel special because I was being highlighted in the group. Abby didn't have a formal "pyramid" back then, but she was big on favoritism—a fact that wasn't lost on the parents whose kids were never chosen for special numbers or spotlight parts.

I was still riding the wave of having Abby's attention when everything came crashing down. The spring before *Dance Moms* started filming, right before school let out, Granddad picked me up from school, got me my McDonald's, and dropped me off at dance, as was our normal routine. But during rehearsal, something very not normal happened: My legs started to hurt.

I sat out for a bit, resting in the back of Studio B, hoping my legs would start to feel better. But after a while I realized I needed to go home. The discomfort in my legs had accelerated from a tired, achy sensation to a pain I couldn't understand. My dad was called, and he came to pick me up early, which was rare. Dancers never left class early. Even when we were sick or hurt, we'd still go to dance to watch in the back of the room, unless things were truly dire. My parents made me an appointment for the following morning with my pediatrician, and I went to bed, hoping I could sleep it off.

By the time I woke up the next morning, both my legs were stinging and tingling, making it difficult for me to stand, much less walk. My mom had left town for her monthly weekend at the University of Pennsylvania, which was a requirement of the doctorate program she'd been working on, so my dad took me to my doctor's appointment. My dad had to carry me from the house to the car and from the car to the doctor's office. Once I'd finished explaining my symptoms to the pediatrician, she immediately told us to go to the hospital.

I was so afraid because hospitals are scary and my mom wasn't there to comfort me. Plus, I had no idea why I was hurting. I was surrounded by sick people who were screaming, crying, or bleeding, making me even more nervous about the testing and evaluations I would undergo.

As soon as Dad told Mom what was happening, she flew back and got to the hospital just in time for my MRI. The doctors poked and prodded at me, trying to figure out the cause of the pain, contributing to my fear of needles. After several tests with no clear results, the medical staff was just as confused as we were. A healthy eight-year-old child does not stop walking overnight. How could this have happened? What exactly had happened? The pain had seemingly come out of nowhere.

Since various tests came back negative, I was sent home, but the pain didn't go away. We returned a short time later, and when the doctors couldn't figure out the problem, one actually accused me of being dishonest. Straight to my face, he said, "There's nothing wrong with you. You're lying." My mom was horrified.

The doctor furthered his accusation by saying I lied because my mom was working too much and I was trying to get attention. My mother told him to put that in writing as the reason to deny my care. For that doctor to be so presumptuous and disrespectful while I was clearly in pain was unacceptable. The accusation was unfathomable; I was not the type of child who would make up an injury, especially if it meant I couldn't dance.

Eventually, I was diagnosed with RND, which stands for Reflex Neurovascular Dystrophy (now known as Complex Regional Pain Syndrome, or CRPS). It's a misunderstood condition in which synapses in the brain misfire and send pain signals to parts of your body. The body responds, and you feel pain, even though you aren't injured. One of the many problems with this disease is that you look perfectly fine on the outside—there are no visual symptoms of looking sick—but you are battling the most unimaginable pain. Scientists have equated it to amputation or childbirth. It is diagnosed by a process of elimination, which can take a long time, and the disorder is rare. However, I learned that teenage girls were more predisposed to getting it, which I found interesting. Even more interesting, they were typically physically active athletes with type-A personalities. I was on the young side of most patients diagnosed with the condition, but I otherwise fit these descriptors to a T.

My case was highly irregular. Typically, flare-ups would be located in one area and sometimes a second on the same side. Mine was occurring on both sides of my body, making the pain even more severe and debilitating.

The doctors mentioned that my condition could have worsened so quickly due to stress. We often don't realize that many of our ailments are caused by mental anguish. If anything, knowing I had RND made me stress out even more.

To keep my muscles from atrophying, I started outpatient physical therapy. It was grueling, and my condition was not improving. In fact, I felt like I was getting worse. The caress of a light breeze set off a sensation of daggers shooting through the soles of my feet. I could not have any blankets on my lower body because it hurt to have the material touch my skin. I definitely could not wear shoes, and socks were out of the question. All fabrics burned like fire. Even now, I am highly sensitive to certain materials.

During this period, I was in and out of the hospital. I had a favorite teacher and was so sad to miss out on the last few weeks of school because of the pain. I did manage to attend our Moving Up day, but I had to use a wheelchair. My classmates didn't understand why I had the wheelchair, and some of them made fun of me. I couldn't comprehend why they were being so cruel; the wheelchair gave me mobility and freedom. What was funny about that?

We were fortunate that Pittsburgh had an in-person treatment center for RND, as these were rare. The incredible Children's Institute facility included dedicated spaces for a hospital, a school, physical therapy, and other treatment programs for physical and behavioral health. The RND program was top-tier and highly specialized. I had to relinquish my wheelchair as soon as I arrived for the in-person program. The daily schedule was packed with exercises—both physical and mental. I am so grateful that I entered this program before my muscles atrophied. I still lost a lot of muscle tone, but I persevered.

The physical exercises were painful. To walk the hallway felt like running a marathon. Just treading water in the pool felt like a win. I was used to the rigors of dance class, but as it turned out, learning how to walk, skip, jump, and swim all over again while managing excruciating pain was harder than anything I'd done before. Interestingly, the program was easier on my mental and emotional health. There were no teachers yelling at me or disregarding my worth. I felt valued by the people who pushed me, and because I felt valued, I knew I was capable of so much more. That was one of the first times I realized the power of a teacher.

Interactions with parents were limited. It is hard for parents to see their children in pain. I think that's why parents could only visit us for short periods of time. My parents loved me so much that they were willing to watch me grow and learn from afar. And the experience taught me so much. I learned that I could do anything I put my mind to. I learned about my personal strength, identified when I needed to ask for help, and advocated for myself. I think it was this experience that most prepared me for the hard work I'd experience on *Dance Moms*.

Part of my treatment was learning strategies to cope with the pain and to prevent flare-ups. As a dancer, you are taught to dance through pain, but this is not necessarily a healthy approach for me. When I get riled up, I have to settle myself and quiet my thinking to avoid a flare-up. When I'm feeling pain, I have to slow down and evaluate whether I'm actually injured or experiencing a temporary discomfort. *Is this pain really bad?* I ask myself. *Are you hurt?* Once I know these answers, I can move forward with a solution. As a dancer, this meant that if I had a cramp, I'd take something for it or massage the area. I'd ice my knee if I moved it the wrong way. I took pain seriously and tended to it instead of pushing through. Eventually, I learned to control as much of my thoughts and actions as possible. I trained my mind to assess and not panic unless there was a serious problem or injury.

Slowly, thanks to the help of physical therapy and this mental shift, I made progress in managing my symptoms. Even now, if I'm tired after a long day or feeling stressed, my legs start tingling, and I have to remind myself to take deep breaths, lie down, and relax. It's a lot easier to deal with as an adult; trying to remember these strategies as a child was hard. After my two-week stay at the in-patient program, I spent the rest of the summer in outpatient treatment and missed dance class, booty camp, and everything else I usually looked forward to. I desperately wanted to get back to the old Nia—to be able to run, jump, and play with my brothers as I always did. Most of all, I wanted to dance. I couldn't wait to get my life back.

The summer ended, and it was finally time to return to school and dance in the fall of 2010. I was nervous that it would be hard to reacclimate to my routine after so much time away. How much had I missed out on?

As it turned out, a lot. Over at the ALDC, I quickly discovered that my team was no longer at the level it was when I had left. While disappointing, this made sense. The thing that didn't make sense was discovering most of the girls I'd danced with were now gone. Before my absence, there had been about eighteen girls in our troupe. Now, we were down to five: Maddie Ziegler, Paige Hyland (the younger sister of Brooke Hyland, whom I'd admired so much), Chloé, me, and a new girl who had joined, Kennedy Trent. Where did everyone go? It was weird that so many people had left in such a short period of time. I'd heard some dancers had moved on to different studios while others had stopped dancing altogether. Though I felt confused and disoriented, I tried not to focus on this change. Instead, I allowed myself to be happy that I was finally back with my friends, back to some form of normalcy.

Only, things weren't normal. I started to feel left behind, like I'd been shoved in the back corner. While my dance technique had regressed during my absence and recovery, the other girls had advanced. I was playing a cruel game of catch-up on a visual stage, and there was a lot to learn. Over the summer, the girls had been taught side aerials and turns. Since most were right-handed, their "good side" was the right, and choreography catered to their strengths accordingly. Though I'm right-handed, my turns and tricks are stronger on the left. As a lefty, I not only had to learn the skill but also be able to do it on my weaker side.

I spent the rest of the season trying to salvage all that was lost. I no longer had Abby's attention and constantly felt forgotten. On the show, my RND would be summed up as something that came and went, mentioned in just a single episode, but it took me more than a year to get back on track.

The first solo I received after my recovery was to Shakira's song "Waka Waka." I loved this fun and energetic jazz routine to a song I enjoyed. I had a cute unitard costume with lots of rhinestones on it, and I got to do tons of tumbling. Having the solo helped me feel that I was finally back to where I'd left off. For this third solo, however, I started to wonder if the song choice was because of my race. It was the official song for the 2010 FIFA World Cup, held in South Africa. It seemed like whenever Abby heard *Africa*, she automatically thought of me.

Time seemed to fly by, and soon the holiday season had passed. When we returned to the studio in January 2011, I was surprised to see flyers announcing that a production company was coming in to do interviews with the dancers and their moms for a potential documentary. We had to audition by submitting a tape of ourselves dancing, and then, if selected, the dancer and her mother would return for an in-person interview with the producer. It was clear that not everyone would be a part of the show, but when I heard about this, I was so excited. It sounded like an amazing opportunity. And what kid wouldn't want to be featured on TV with her friends? Later, we learned the concept of the show was to highlight dance moms and their daughters and the drama that happens behind the scenes.

I asked my parents a few times if I could audition, but they weren't sure. This sort of thing just didn't happen in Pittsburgh, which is less glamorous than other cities, so they weren't sure the opportunity was legitimate and not some sort of scam. It didn't help that, at this time, there were countless contests advertised on the radio or television claiming to be able to help children become the next star—for a price, of course.

But we soon learned the reason behind the opportunity. Apparently, Abby had been complaining about the moms to a friend, John Corella, who knew a producer named Bryan Stinson. John spoke with Bryan about what he'd learned from Abby, and together they created a concept for the show. By the time the audition flyers were hanging in the dance studio, the show had supposedly already been picked up by Lifetime.

There was nothing particularly spectacular about our dance studio. We were in middle-of-nowhere Pennsylvania, in a residential neighborhood. Perhaps that was part of the charm. *You can find a star anywhere in America!* the show seemed to promise. *Maybe even in your own backyard or in your classroom sitting next to you.*

Though they had some reservations, my parents finally agreed to let me try out. We compiled clips from my performances, and my mom was invited to schedule our interview. She was working on her dissertation for her doctorate at the time and was still the principal of the middle and elementary school, so it took a little finagling to find a slot that would work.

The interview with Bryan Stinson was held in Studio B. Mom and I sat down across from him and had a simple conversation. Mom had let me do my own makeup, so I had glitter all over my face, plus a tiara on my head, and I was wearing the costume from my "Nattie of the Jungle" performance.

The interview wasn't very long. "Why do you love dance?" Bryan asked. "What are your goals?" He wanted us to tell him more about life at the studio. Of course, my dream had always been to win a crown, so I mentioned it. He loved the idea that I had this fixation on winning a title. He also wanted to know how my mom felt about my relationship with the other girls, and he wanted to get a sense for the depth of her relationship with the other moms. The interview concluded with him asking us about Abby and what it was like working with her. We were candid in saying that Abby had a habit of typecasting me, but it was just an offhand remark. Abby really wasn't a focal point in the beginning. In fact, Bryan seemed more interested in the fact that I was distracted by the stink bugs crawling around, something he remembered long after that moment.

Afterward, I remember getting in the car with my mom to head home. We sat there, waiting to pull out of the parking lot, when she turned to me and said, "Hey, Nia, before you get your hopes up, I just need to let you know that they're not going to pick us. We're just too boring." We'd heard they were meeting with other dance studios and had narrowed it down to ours and a studio in California.

"It's okay if we don't make it," I assured her. "At least we tried."

About a month later, I sat at the table eating dinner with my family—Hamburger Helper, I think—when we got a call on our landline. I answered the phone and was shocked to hear Bryan Stinson on the other line. He said, "Hey, we would love to have you on our show. We're gonna call it *Just Dance*." He went on to tell me that two people had already committed, and they wanted to know if I would say yes too.

"Oh my gosh!" I replied. "This is so exciting!" I called my mom over and stunned her with the news.

"This doesn't even seem real," she said as we hugged each other. I was oblivious to her trepidations. My face lit up in the biggest smile.

I sat back at the table to finish my dinner. The Hamburger Helper tasted extra good that night.

3 Show Business

The first contract we signed with Lifetime was for six weeks. The cast consisted of myself and my mom; Maddie and Mackenzie Ziegler and their mom, Melissa; Chloé and her mom, Christi; Paige and Brooke Hyland and their mom, Kelly; and then a girl who wasn't from the studio, Vivi-Anne Stein and her mother, Cathy. Though the original agreement was for a short period of time, there was a clause that extended the term to seven seasons—the longest time you can contract someone for work in this business—if the series was picked up.

To be fair, our attorney did warn us that it was a bad contract. There was nothing in it that protected the talent. We had no rights to the content and could not use or say anything in correlation with the show without the network's approval. It also stated our salary for the duration of the show, which was less than $1,000 a week for the both of us before taxes. We were not in the driver's seat, and it would be a while before we could amend the contract. Over time we learned more about the business and were able to renegotiate some terms, but it was never an ideal agreement.

In the beginning, though, we thought we were signing a contract for a six-week documentary. What did we have to lose? Besides, we didn't have time to sit and think on it; the network gave us only one day to review and commit. If we said no, they would move on to the next person on the list.

Upon seeing the contract and discussing it with our attorney, my mom quickly called the other girls' parents, and they spoke about the terms. Everyone had the same agreement. My parents explained the contract to me as best they could, but I was only nine years old. I wasn't paying attention to the legalities of anything. I only knew that I wanted to be a star, to be on TV; I wanted to dance and travel with my friends. My mom was a little hesitant but followed my lead. She was always trying to instill in us freedom of choice and decision-making. My parents were giving me my first dose of independence and sense of self. She did, however, say, "If you do this, you have to honor this commitment."

I could barely wait for her to finish her sentence before I nodded my head yes.

We agreed to the terms and signed.

A production crew came out to the studio each day to film our rehearsals. My parents had to renegotiate their schedules, since filming would start immediately after school ended.

With the start of the show came the inception of our ranking system. The original system was called "Chalkboard," and to us kids, it was exciting seeing our headshots on display. "Pyramid" evolved over time once we started to travel and could not bring the chalkboard with us.

At the conclusion of filming for the six weeks, the network decided to opt in to a series and extended our six weeks of production to thirteen. They had struck gold with the cast. You could not find a more dysfunctional group of people, and they weren't about to let us slip away. We now had an official season 1 of a show that had been renamed *Dance Moms.*

It was all fun and games at first, but there was a major culture shift as the seasons progressed. The ALDC was no longer a fun place where we could express ourselves through our cute outfits or makeup. It became very serious and, with every season, more grueling. Our dance clothes no longer showed our personalities. This was Abby's doing. She would tell us not to draw attention to ourselves because we would stand out in a negative way. I can still hear her say, "Nia, you're always a beat behind. Don't draw attention to yourself with your outfit or your hair. You need to blend in." Over time those comments started to impact me. Little by little, my light was dimmed.

As we got older, Abby started to make us all wear the same color or outfits, or even her own merch to promote her brand. Initially we were excited to be wearing a team uniform, but we later realized we were walking billboards for her merch brand—free labor.

The pyramid became a symbol of power, and it had a tremendous impact on our lives. It was a visual representation of popularity and social capital, conveying even more than Abby's words. And its impact reached beyond the dance studio. On social media, people took up the same mindset, reciting verbatim things that were said during pyramid, commenting on my perceived weaknesses since I was always on the bottom.

This placement even had repercussions when it came to booking jobs. Was someone on the bottom a desirable candidate? I was finding that the answer was no. Being on the bottom of the pyramid was like having a failing grade or low ranking at school, and it restricted access to certain opportunities. Being invited to auditions, securing direct books, finding representation in top agencies, getting invitations to events and premieres—all were impacted by how you were positioned.

Pyramid days took place every Tuesday, and we would also film every Wednesday, Thursday, and Friday. Fridays we traveled to our competitions, then we'd come back on Sunday for a brief respite before starting it all again. The schedule being what it was, I missed just about every Friday of school. Instead of attending classes, us dancers and our moms would meet at the studio and load up all our gear onto a smelly charter bus to head wherever our event was being held. Once we arrived, we'd settle into our hotel, then the next day jump right into competition. You can imagine how exhausted I was returning to school on Monday without any real rest over the weekend. I also often missed out on birthday parties, family gatherings, or get-togethers, but to me the trade-off—the fun of the dance competitions—was worth it.

Traveling was a key component to my *Dance Moms* experience, and so much of my life happened on the bus. We would go to places like Virginia, New York, New Jersey, and Ohio, making our rides really long sometimes. I would try to do my schoolwork to distract me but inevitably ended up talking to the other girls, working on rainbow loom bracelets, or watching movies. I typically sat next to Kenzie, the youngest dancer on the team. We were both often overlooked by the other girls and would get paired up by default. I sometimes put my bag on a seat early to choose a good seat, hoping that one of the other girls might want to sit next to me, but my bag would always be moved to the seat Kenzie and I usually sat in. The only time this truly crushed me was when I found one of the straps on my Louis Vuitton tote bag broken. It had been a gift from my parents, and one not easily replaced.

Despite the disappointing circumstances of our pairing, I truly enjoyed hanging out with Kenzie, and we became the best of friends. We had so much in common because I wasn't in a rush to grow up like some of the other girls. They were more into being older like Brooke and they didn't really play with stuffed animals or watch cartoons. But Kenzie did those things with me, and I loved it. I could be myself and not be considered babyish.

Still, I can't pretend like it didn't hurt my feelings that the other girls cliqued up and didn't choose to sit next to me. Dance had been the one place where I felt like I fit in, but week after week, I was slowly discovering that my place at the bottom of the pyramid was impacting not only my professional opportunities but also my social capital. If anything, this made me more determined to work hard and get better. Then maybe Abby and the other girls would pick me.

Something I hear often is that people think our dance competitions on the show were faked or rigged. But that couldn't have been further from the truth. Everything we did or went through for those competitions was absolutely real. What I will say is that a lot of the major dance competitions did not want *Dance Moms* to film there. They thought that the film crew following us around impeded the other competitors. So, after two seasons, we realized that traditional dance competitions were not going to work well with our production schedule.

The reasons for this stretched beyond unwanted notoriety from the show. Most of the competitions were actually dance conventions, so before our competitive performances, we attended a full day of classes, including jazz, contemporary, ballet, hip-hop, and tap. We would also work with different choreographers to learn dance combinations that we'd then perform in groups.

Each day followed a strict schedule, usually broken down by age and performance type. Someone could have a solo at eight o'clock in the morning and then a group dance at noon; then another group dance or trio might take place later in the evening. Awards and announcements often didn't occur until after everyone had performed and could begin as late as eleven o'clock at night. The production crew, however, had a cutoff time; they couldn't be there to film us 24/7. They had a budget to adhere to. That meant competition directors were required to make special accommodations for us, like moving the schedule around so we could do our routines within a certain window of time or switching audience members' seats so our moms, the teachers, and Abby could be sitting close to the front. We disrupted the flow, and other attendees resented the fact that we were given so much leeway in the schedule.

Some might be surprised to learn that our performances during competition were filmed twice. The first time we performed was for adjudication, when the judges would score our routines. If there were solos, duets, or trios, we would each perform them back-to-back. Then the judges would leave the room so we could perform a second time, just for the cameras. The only performance that counted for awards was the first one. We had one shot at winning, just like every other contestant. In some ways, our chances of winning were even slimmer than other competitors' because, while many of them competed the same numbers throughout the year, we had to learn new ones each week for the show. We had one time to compete the dance, and that was it.

We usually had a moment to catch our breath in between the first performance and the next time we had to go out onstage. It was not uncommon for the second performance to be better than the first. We'd gotten the jitters out by then and had an opportunity to run the dance full-out onstage as opposed to in rehearsal. The second time around was easier and more relaxed because there were no scores and we were more familiar with the space. We just had to make sure we did not make any glaring errors or have a wardrobe malfunction—mistakes we knew would be used in the episode. One time, I landed a front aerial beautifully in the first performance of one of my solos, but the second time I stumbled out of it. Of course that was the version used on the show. It was TV gold to feature a mistake—and a great opportunity for Abby to yell at you for messing up.

Needless to say, our presence wasn't convenient for anyone there—the other competitors, the judges, and the audience alike. We also tended to make the other competitors uncomfortable. The film crew of mostly men—the camera guy, sound guy, and sometimes the associate director or producer—would follow us backstage as well as to other areas, where dancers might have been getting changed or were not fully dressed. Though the crew was never allowed into the main dressing room, some dancers have to do quick costume changes or deal with wardrobe malfunctions, so it can get a bit weird if there are grown men walking around.

Due to these factors, after the first couple of seasons, we were asked not to attend some of the bigger, more popular competitions. So Lifetime and the production company had to look into smaller dance competitions for us to compete at. Sometimes events were created and managed by established dance competitions to allow for filming. Studios were invited to participate with a limited number of entries available so we could stick to the daily film schedule. While the competitions themselves were created for us, they were still legitimate competitions. The wins and losses were real.

So were our busy schedules. There was a clear separation between filming life and regular studio life—not to mention school life. Once the cameras were turned off, we went back to our regular studio schedule. Some viewers have wondered how this impacted us kids holistically. But I found that I was actually a more focused student amid my busy schedule. The pressure that often accompanied dance kept me focused and built determination and a strong work ethic. Staying busy allowed for fewer distractions because I knew I had a short window to take care of everything on my plate.

Despite the intense routine that filming created, the "OG" members of the cast didn't receive special treatment at the ALDC because we were on a TV show. It was more like the opposite: We were reminded constantly about how grateful we should be. We were humbled at the studio and warned that there were better dancers there—particularly in Abby's senior company. The fact that we were now doing the show and competing every weekend did not give us a pass on anything.

Tales from the Dressing Room

Competition dance is as much about the costumes, hair, and makeup as it is about the actual dancing. I loved that aspect of it. I loved playing with makeup and learning how to do my hair. I also loved beautiful costumes with sparkles and rhinestones, although most of my solo costumes on the show weren't very pretty. They often felt matronly and had so much fabric, which seemed like it was done on purpose. Abby made it clear that my legs—specifically, my thighs and feet—needed to be hidden, so I often had pants or long skirts to conceal them. I hoped and prayed I would get better costumes at some point because all the other girls had gorgeous costumes: beautiful skirts that were above the knee, gorgeous colors, sequins and stones that shined on stage. I dreamed of getting costumes I felt pretty in.

On the hair and makeup side, things weren't much easier. My mom didn't really know how to do hair or makeup. She was a principal—not a hair and makeup artist! Before we started *Dance Moms*, the only makeup I ever saw her wear was lipstick. She did her best, but at a certain point I decided to take over and do my hair and makeup myself.

At first it looked like a ten-year-old had styled herself because, well, one had. But as the years went on, I got better. I learned from the other girls, their moms, and the makeup artist we had on set who primarily did the moms' makeup or our makeup for interviews. I also watched and learned from YouTube videos. It took time, but my skills improved to the point where I could help the other girls with their hair and makeup.

I absolutely loved makeup. I know most kids don't use it when they're still in elementary school, but in the beginning seasons of the show I wore it only for competitions. I didn't start wearing makeup during rehearsals until I was a teenager. I'm grateful my parents let me play around with it as a child. They always reminded me I didn't need makeup, but they saw how much I loved it and knew that it was just another medium of expression and art. They would even get me makeup for Christmases and birthdays. I collected it the same way I collected costumes.

Unfortunately, my makeup and hair seemed to be an issue for Abby. She wanted us to wear the same shade of blush and the same color lipstick for group dances, and sometimes those shades looked different on me. Abby would get mad at me because she thought I was using a different color and trying to stand out, but I literally had to show her I was using the same shade as everyone else. Sometimes I would have to mix different shades together to get a color match. The whole thing felt ridiculous to me because we were onstage, far away from the audience. No one could tell if the shade was slightly off.

Still, Abby was always irritated that I stuck out. My skin tone did not blend in. My hair was different. My eye color and body type didn't fit in with the other girls. According to Abby, my entire appearance made the group less uniform. There would be sighs of exasperation and reminders of what I had to do to make my costumes or shoes work to match my skin tone. Slowly, I began to internalize this negativity and become self-conscious. I had always been vibrant, energetic, and sure of myself, but this type of criticism was damaging for a ten-year-old.

One time, during season 2, I had my hair in braids. It was a protective style, and I received approval from production. (Any major change to our hair color, cut, or style had to be approved by production because of the need for continuity.) Abby told me that I needed to fix my hair because it looked awful. She said—on camera, no less—"It's like a log coming out of the side of her head."[1]

Once, in rehearsal, Abby asked me, "Don't you just wish you had white-girl hair?"

I was taken aback by her question, but I responded, "No."

"Oh, really?" she said, "Like, don't you just think it'd be so much easier?"

Again, I told her no. It didn't matter what she said—I knew I didn't want to be white. Unlike the other exchange, this one never aired.

These are just a few examples of my conversations with Abby when it came to my hair. Typically, the direction for hairstyles was straight, so I was constantly straightening my hair, which put a strain on it. Although braids were the easiest and best choice for me, Abby didn't allow me to have them. Most of the hairstyles chosen for us were almost impossible to accomplish with braids.

We also used tons of products, like gels and hairsprays, to slick back our hair into tight buns and French twists. Abby; her assistant, Gianna; and even my teammates did not understand how difficult this was for me. Hair was something I had to plan for in advance, something that the other girls did not have to worry about. I needed to have the right products to achieve certain looks, and if I didn't have them, I was out of luck. Doing my hair was not a simple wash-and-go situation. I might even need to make a hair appointment to do something as simple as getting it flat ironed. But to others, my hair care needs were nothing more than an unnecessary distraction.

"Hey," I would ask early in the week, trying to be proactive, "what's the hairstyle this weekend?"

"Why are you asking this now?" Abby or Gianna would respond. "Just worry about the dance."

After getting yelled at so many times, I tried my best to keep my hair in a state where it could easily be manipulated without too much damage. But there were some suggested styles I couldn't prepare for no matter how hard I tried.

"We're gonna have wet hair for this dance," Abby announced once, out of the blue.

"Wet hair"? Wait a minute. What do you mean by "wet hair"? Like, what look are you going for because my wet hair doesn't look the same as the other girls' wet hair. I never had a relaxer, so if I got my hair wet, there was a strong chance that the resulting curls would not be conducive to the expected style. So the wet look became another style Abby could not do because my hair would not do what she wanted. According to her, my hair was limiting her artistic freedom.

And she wasn't the only one who was unhappy. Other girls would also be excited to do something fun and different with their hair and then be inevitably disappointed because it wasn't possible for me. I felt like I was holding them back or being an inconvenience by just existing and being realistic about my appearance.

We were also required to wear elaborate headpieces for many of our dances. We had an irrational fear of impending danger if a headpiece were to fall off onstage during competition. We'd previously used bobby pins or a darning needle and thread to secure the headpieces, but they would still sometimes slip off. So we resorted to a new method of securing them to our heads—really, to our scalps: zip ties. Yes, one of the hair and makeup artists on set, who was incredibly clever in adapting to any situation or wardrobe crisis, developed the zip-tie method. We would line up one by one and have any item zip-tied that we worried might fall off.

Zip ties were not the most comfortable, and they put a strain on your scalp, so I wouldn't recommend it to others. Still, the zip ties did their job! We never had a headpiece malfunction when using them. They did, however, result in hair breakage. Whether it was due to the pulling of the hair on the scalp or cutting out pieces when removing the zip ties from our hair, they left casualties in their wake. Often, I would get awful headaches from the ties being too tight, or my scalp would be raw and bleeding because of them, but I worried less about that and more about having a stellar performance—which meant no wardrobe malfunctions. As they say, no pain, no gain.

I remember one time James Washington, who was a teacher at Abby's studio, choreographed a beautiful number for me, and Abby had me wear a white head wrap. This was prior to the zip-tie method. My mom and Chloé's mom attempted to sew it in with the darning needle, but it still felt loose. I told my mom it wasn't secure, but we'd run out of time, and she assured me it would be fine. About halfway through my performance, it slipped backward, and although it didn't fall off, the fact that it slipped out of position was just as bad. The bottom part was still attached, but the top part was hanging off the back of my head. Abby didn't yell at me—but boy, was I mad at myself. I had a complete meltdown after I got offstage. Fans probably thought it was funny and kind of silly, but for me, it felt like the end of the world. From that point on, I would do anything to keep my headpieces on. Bobby pins and thread just weren't enough.

To help us keep all our getting-ready supplies in one place, the network gave us ginormous makeup bags that looked more like carry-on suitcases than makeup organizers. They were wheeled and had all sorts of compartments and drawers. Inside, we stored tons of makeup, bobby pins of various colors and sizes, safety pins, needles and thread, hair pieces, extensions and wigs, curlers, and hair ties. We were on cloud nine. This was our first experience getting gifted items, and I loved it.

Abby, though, resented us receiving this gift and complained to production that we did not need them. She had a tantrum—one of many over the years—regarding the special treatment we received. This would be an ongoing issue. If fans sent us fan mail to the studio, she would keep it and claim that we did not need anything. We would see stuffed animals and other little trinkets and artwork collected by her and never given to their intended recipients.

In the end, we resorted to suitcases as our competition bags. The makeup bags had been a nice gesture, but we needed the extra space a suitcase allowed for all the things we accumulated—like dance shoes. I had various types of shoes as well as multiple pairs of the same exact shoe. We went through shoes quickly because once they got dirty, we weren't allowed to wear them onstage. Abby's theory was that the dirt would distract the judges and make them look at our feet instead of at the dance as a whole. We also had extra shoes in case of emergency.

I had to dye my shoes because of my skin tone. We would use foundation to match my complexion, which took a lot of time and a lot of foundation. But light-colored shoes against my skin would have definitely drawn attention to my feet, and Abby certainly wouldn't want that. She always criticized me for having "bad feet." In dancer lingo, this is code for not having strong arches and pointed toes, and it's one of the worst criticisms a dancer can get. The thing about having "bad feet" is, it's not something that can be fixed overnight, nor is it something that happens for lack of trying. It takes a long time to train your feet to hold the proper position. Abby's repeated orders to fix my feet only amplified the narrative that I was a poor or weak dancer. I did exercises regularly to strengthen and lengthen the muscles and ligaments, but my feet were not designed the optimal way for dancing.

Having different feet would not have solved all my problems. Abby believed that Black people were physically predisposed to have flat feet. She would say, "Well, you know your people have flat feet. You know, because you're African American and they have flat feet." This struck me as ignorant; I know plenty of Black dancers with perfectly arched feet! Yet, despite the fact that she actually believed this ridiculous generalization was true, she'd threaten punishment for my perceived shortcoming. "If you don't point that foot," she'd warn, "I'm gonna come out there and break it."

I wanted so badly to have the perfect arch and toe point that I wrote to Santa to tell him I wanted good feet for Christmas. When I told Nana (my mom's mom) about this wish, she said, "What? You have beautiful feet! What would make you say that? Nothing is wrong with your feet." But I never stopped working on them.

The criticisms about my body were wide-reaching, though, and felt relentless. Comments came directly from Abby and trickled down to some of the girls and their moms, criticizing my thighs, my butt, and even my muscular legs. I wasn't frail or lean like many of my counterparts, so this was just one more unacceptable way that I stood out in Abby's eyes. She frequently called me fat, pointing out my big butt and hips. Her harsh criticism was then broadcast on the show for the world to see.

As I got older, things got worse. At one point in season 6, Abby talked about the size of my thighs in the dressing room. She implied that I was fat because I was not working hard enough.[2] This was just one of many comments Abby made to create an illusion that I was lazy or just not strong as a dancer. Viewers and some of my castmates ate that up without question. Since Abby said it, it must be true. Of course, my mom called Abby out on that lie again. I had trained over the break—just not at Abby's studio. I took a ballet intensive at Debbie Allen Dance Academy, featuring Misty Copeland and Complexions Contemporary Ballet.

This body shaming was hurtful. Even more hurtful was the fact that none of the moms aside from my own came to my defense when Abby body-shamed me. I couldn't help but think it was because they agreed with her. It's no wonder America believed I was worthy of the bottom of the pyramid. It felt like there was nothing I could do to counter the image that Abby's words amplified.

I hadn't been in the room when Abby made that comment about my thighs and wasn't told about it. I also didn't watch the show (really!). So I was confused and blindsided when, after the episode aired, I started seeing comments, tweets, and texts about the conversation—most of them defending me and telling me not to listen to Abby. Others were mean about my body. It was horrifying to learn that my appearance was being talked about on TV. I was a teenager going through puberty on a very public stage, so I was constantly trying to hide my body, covering myself up out of insecurity and in an attempt to avoid further scrutiny. I actually started the trend of wearing Lululemon at the dance studio because I was always wearing Lululemon leggings and other girls started to wear them too. I also wore tank tops instead of crop tops to cover my stomach. You can imagine how uncomfortable I was when my body became a featured part of the *Dance Moms* discussion. Even the kind and supportive comments unnerved me.

One text I received was from an influencer I knew well, Gabbie Hanna. She said, "Don't listen to her. Thick thighs save lives." She was right, but at the time her comment made me feel worse because she seemed to be agreeing that my thighs were thick. Eventually, I learned to embrace my natural curves. But back then, I was young, unsure of myself and how I was developing. The moms and even Abby would comment on how beautiful the other girls were in their costumes or makeup, at rehearsals and competitions. Meanwhile, the narrative about my appearance was tainted with criticism. My beauty was not seen by others, so it was difficult for me to see it myself.

Dancers are often susceptible to body dysmorphia because they are constantly holding themselves to such strict standards. I mean, you're *always* looking in the mirror. And what the mirror showed me was that I had hips, a butt, and breasts, no matter how much I worked out or trained. Then I was forced to put that body into super-skimpy costumes, which were another point of contention.

Many of our costumes on the show were not actual costumes. A lot of them came from department stores like Justice, Macy's, and Target, and were then enhanced with appliqués and rhinestones. In general, they consisted of some type of bra or crop top and shorts. We used lingerie as costumes as well. Once in a while we would get actual dance costumes from a catalog or have a costume handmade by someone, but those were rare.

Aside from the costumes being skimpy, I was bothered that Abby always made me wear yellow. "Black people look good in yellow," she would say. "It looks good on your skin." So even though my favorite color was pink, I was forever stuck in yellow or orange.

Since we never knew what our costumes were going to be, I would have anxiety waiting to see what was planned. Sometimes we wouldn't find out what we were wearing until the day of the competition. The anxiety went up tenfold if I had my period. Imagine wearing a leotard with no tights and feeling that familiar sensation of your cycle flowing. For reasons like this, the girls and I would often joke that we were more afraid to perform onstage for a live audience than we were when filming for the show.

5

At the Bottom

Our pyramid days moved from Tuesday to Wednesday, and because of this, Wednesdays became the worst days ever. This was not a time for us to laugh and joke and speak constructively about our dancing and how we could improve. Instead, it was an opportunity for Abby to personally attack each of us—especially the girls who ranked at the bottom, like me. It felt like torture. We would have to stand in front of the big mirror for literally three hours while Abby talked and talked: criticizing us, telling us about our next event or dance routines, or sharing anything else she felt she needed to say to fill the time.

And then, in the background, the moms would be arguing about one thing or another. The fact that someone's daughter didn't get chosen for a solo or a lead in a group dance, or whether an instructor was out of line for how they spoke to someone's child. No one wanted to go against Abby to voice a difference of opinion. To do so was like declaring war on your child in future episodes. Although Abby didn't have full creative control, she definitely had influence over the dances. She would fight with production regarding the themes and dig in her heels about who would get a solo or duets or trios. Abby could pull you from a dance number without any particular reason. I was pulled from more than one dance because Abby got into an argument with my mom.

Pyramid episodes took up our entire production time on Wednesdays and were primarily a device for the show. After a while, it became monotonous; I was frequently at the bottom, Maddie at the top.

Anyone who has seen *Dance Moms* knows that Maddie is an incredible dancer who deserves all her accolades. She was also Abby's favorite, so she received the most and best solos. In season 4, she became a breakout star for being featured in Sia's music video for her song "Chandelier" and then was the face of Sia for years to come. Opportunity after opportunity came her way.

Maddie is a hard worker, but she also had certain advantages that the rest of us weren't afforded. For example, because she was homeschooled early on, she sometimes got to learn choreography before the rest of us. It was frustrating when Abby would criticize the rest of us on-camera for not being able to pick up choreography as quickly as Maddie or not refining our movements the way Maddie did, when she'd had more time to perfect the dances. And the truth is, Maddie *is* a fast learner, so she didn't need the extra time anyway.

After *Dance Moms* ended and I had some time to reflect, I started to wonder whether the whole point of the show had been to make Maddie a star. Abby favored Maddie, and production seemed to cater to what Abby wanted. It was hurtful to look back and realize I was never going to get the same opportunities Maddie had, no matter how hard I worked or how long I stayed. To a degree, it felt like the rest of us dancers were expendable, pawns in Abby's game and innocent bystanders in the drama between the moms.

At any rate, it wasn't long before the dynamic was established: Maddie was the prodigy, and I was the weak link. I was no longer just happy to be competing with my friends and traveling the country as I'd been during our first season of filming, no longer having fun with this new adventure. The perception—shared by Abby, the moms, the viewers, and even some of the other girls—was that I was no threat or competition to anyone on the team. I hadn't allowed that opinion to steal my joy, but it had dulled my shine.

I don't think I was able to shed this perception even when the dance studio moved to LA. I remember clearly not being picked for a trio because, I was told, I could not turn (which wasn't true). No one wants to be the kid chosen last for the team, but how are you supposed to feel when you're not chosen for the team at all? Though she'd developed a reputation for being blunt and hurtful, Abby was not always forthcoming when she didn't want me in a dance. She would make up a reason, like my costume was "lost" when it was not. Still, I put on a brave face. I knew my potential even if others did not see it.

Yet, no matter how hurt I was, I was always taught by Abby to hold in my emotions and not cry—because crying meant weakness. She often told us, "Save your tears for the pillow," and she ingrained into our heads that crying in front of someone made you a loser. Sometimes if I felt like I needed to cry during filming, I'd try to hide in the bathroom to collect myself. But that wasn't truly a safe space; if a crew member turned out to be in there and heard me being upset, I'd come out of the bathroom to find a camera in my face, capturing my distress. Sometimes they'd even film *inside* the bathroom, if no one else was in there.

That's why there were very few times I was seen crying on the show. Notably, one of the only times I did cry was because my grandad, who used to take me to dance, was sick. To this day, I still have a hard time letting myself cry, even though I understand it's a healthy part of being human.

Season 3 was when I started to really feel the weight of being at the bottom of the pyramid week after week. Because I was at the bottom, I wasn't getting granted the same opportunities as the other girls—or even any opportunity to showcase what I brought to the team. I was shoved in the back of group dances and strategically hidden behind other dancers. Even the girls themselves were starting to buy into the narrative; I remember another teammate, Kendall Vertes (who had joined the team back in season 2), rolling her eyes whenever she found out we were paired for a duet together. To see firsthand that someone didn't want to dance with me really, really stung. Worst of all, being at the bottom meant there was no room for me to grow. I went seven months without being given a solo. That's a long time when you go to dance competitions every weekend.

As the seasons passed, it started clicking in my head that I genuinely wasn't wanted on the team. At first, I'd thought I had to work my way up and prove myself, but after working my butt off and improving season by season and still not getting any sort of reward for all my hard work, it hit me that I'd been pigeonholed as a weak dancer, and I couldn't escape that narrative. Instead of walking away, though, I decided to buckle down and work even harder. Whether or not Abby thought I was talented, I could at least show her my growth. Not having a solo gave me more time to work on my technique, stretch, and get ahead on schoolwork. I was making the most of my situation.

The frustrating thing was that even before the show started, I'd often place in the top five with my solos, but at the ALDC the mentality was that "second place is the first to lose." If you didn't win first place, you lost—and that meant you were a loser. In a healthy environment, a top-five placement would have been seen as both a success and an opportunity for growth. But to Abby, it was a failure. There is nothing wrong with failure. That is how you grow. How you respond to failure is what matters. What are you learning? What do you do so you are not making the same mistakes? How do you showcase growth? At school you have tests or quizzes where you can demonstrate a skill set and see where you need to improve. That's what competition should be. I do not agree with the stigma attached to failure. Without the experience of competition, how was I going to get better as a soloist onstage? I was not entitled. I was a student who wanted more from her dance education. I wanted the same opportunity that was afforded to others: to learn appropriate, challenging choreography and be given a time to showcase what I did best. I wanted to dance with joy and freedom without fear of being ridiculed or bashed.

This last desire should have been a given—especially during rehearsals. Rehearsals are like homework, a place where you can make mistakes and figure things out. The stakes are not the same as they are during a competition. Rehearsal should be viewed as a learning environment. And you know what's not conducive to learning? Being so uptight and on edge about making a mistake that you can't perform—and knowing that every misstep would be filmed and could be used to further a negative narrative about me. People are quick to criticize that I was a beat behind here or there, but to them I say: How would you feel in my shoes, knowing there was a dragon breathing down your neck, ready to criticize any imperfection? Would you dance your best?

As I got older and moved into my teenage years, I realized, I wasn't at the bottom because of anything I was (or wasn't) doing. I was there because someone felt like putting me there. It was more of an Abby problem than a me problem. No matter how good I was, I was never going to be at the top of Abby's pyramid. Even if I outperformed everyone else, she'd find one reason or another to put me at the bottom. Sometimes it was because she didn't like something my mom said or did.

Challenging Abby meant you were engaging in battle, so you'd better make sure it was a fight worth fighting. Abby did not play fair and could hold a grudge for a long time. One of my most successful solos was "Goodbye Maya" in season 4, which was a tribute to Maya Angelou. Abby did not choreograph this dance for me; she was mad at my mom due to an argument they'd had in the dressing room during competition the previous week. Anytime one of our moms would get into a disagreement with Abby, she loved to throw in our faces what an amazing opportunity being in her dance school was. "Nobody would know Nia's name if it wasn't for me," she said. When my mom pointed out that her treatment of a little kid (me) was inappropriate, Abby retorted, "Nia is twelve! She can have kids! She can get married in some countries!"[1] It was wildly inappropriate for her to suggest that without her intervention, I'd be just another Black teenage mom. I sensed the racial undertones to her comments, but the most egregious of these were edited out of the show. Abby seemed to think that she was "rescuing" me from the systems of oppression, when she was the one building the walls by scaffolding a series of lies, deceit, and innuendo.

Since Abby refused to work with me that week, I worked with James Washington. James was a wonderful instructor, so I didn't care much that Abby chose not to choreograph for me. I loved this dance because it involved mature choreography. Usually, my solos were watered down, but in this piece I felt like I was actually dancing. It had powerful movements and was also challenging—not only because of the choreography but because I had to recite some spoken word during the dance as well. For this, I had to learn how to control my breathing. I got better as a dancer when I had routines like this, ones that hit the sweet spot between showcasing me and pushing me toward something more. I won first place for this dance—without Abby. It showed me what I could achieve when I worked with a teacher with both compassion and high standards. Best of all, it happened on my thirteenth birthday! Winning was the best present ever.

Controversy and Conflict

Working on reality TV from the age of nine makes you grow up quickly. Things most kids don't even think about become part of your daily life. You have to show up for work and show up on time. In addition to your parents and teachers, you often have more than one boss telling you what to do. You have to be mindful of cameras filming your every move—anything you say or do can be used against you, and you have no control over the editing. You learn to be cautious with your words, actions, and emotions.

I was particularly careful with my words and behaviors because I did not want to be called aggressive, loud, disruptive, or angry. It seemed to me that these loaded terms were usually reserved for Black girls, while my peers were called cute, playful, and excited for exhibiting the same behaviors. There were different rules and standards for different people. If you were on the bottom of the pyramid, you still had to show up for work, but your role was more as background and supporting cast than a potential future star. Your presence was needed but not necessarily valued.

At this young age, I began to notice "office politics" and wonder who I could trust. The short answer turned out to be almost no one. I saw the nuances of relationships and alliances being built, ultimately creating cliques and allegiances—things most kids would never usually see condoned in everyday life. But in the dance world, they were embraced. At school, our motto had been "Think also of the comforts and rights of others." At the ALDC, that sentiment was tossed out the window. People did whatever they could to get ahead. Bullying got disguised as "coaching," and bad behavior was not only tolerated but encouraged. The worse you acted, the more likely you were to get screen time and a storyline.

The "controversial" content of the dances that viewers obsessed over and thought were big deals paled in comparison to the things that really mattered to me as a child growing up in front of the world. The dances were meant to shock and create debate or conversation; I was used to this. Dance is an artistic expression. It is supposed to make people feel something. I think that is why the show was such a hit. It made dance relevant in everyday lives.

I like to believe that we were part of this pop culture phenomenon that revolved not only around competition dance but dance as a whole. There was an increase in the number of students enrolled in dance studios, and dance competition attendance hit record numbers after *Dance Moms* aired. It's wild to see what competition dance is like now. It has changed so much since I first competed on *Dance Moms*. I can't even imagine how our team would do now. We were great in my eyes, but this generation of dancers is at a completely different level. I was part of that, and I am proud of it. But helping to impact the world in this way contributed to the sense of growing up fast.

Gianna Martello—Gia, as we call her—was Abby's assistant. Many people don't know this, but Gia choreographed most of our dances. Abby liked to do the beginning or end of the dances, and she'd add a few steps here and there, but the core of the choreography was left to Gia.

My relationship with Gia evolved over the years. When I was

little, Gia was really hard on me. She would repeat some of the mean things Abby said about my dancing and not being good enough for the group. Even when Abby wasn't in our rehearsals, Gia parroted the same phrases. My mom had to talk to her a few times about the way she spoke to me. It was hard enough to have Abby ridicule me on the daily; I didn't need Gia doing the same.

As I got older and progressed, Gia became fond of my improvement. It took years to get to that place, but, in the later seasons, we ended up having a good rapport and finding mutual respect. In many ways, we matured and grew up together.

I want to give Gia her flowers because she really was the one to make our team what it was. She's very talented, and she worked so hard to keep our dances clean and together. She was the one who stayed at the studio until ten or eleven at night, finishing our dances and calling last-minute rehearsals the night before competition to make sure we were prepared. Even though she wasn't always the kindest to us, she did care about us, and she wanted us to go onstage ready. And I really do appreciate the passion she put into our team. But at the end of the day, I knew where Gia stood: She was still Abby's assistant, and she was always going to be Team Abby.

A lot of the routines choreographed by Abby and Gianna were dark and edgy. There were few subjects that we would not tackle; almost nothing was taboo. I think Abby went this route because it moved the audience, often resulting in wins for us, particularly for our group dances. The lyrics to the song choice for an early routine from season 1, "Where Have All the Children Gone?," told the story of a child's abduction, and the choreography had each of us being "murdered" as we exited the stage. That was one of our most iconic dances due to its subject matter and gruesome nature. I don't think most people in America had seen this type of dance—something that wasn't cute, bubbly, or happy—performed by little girls. It became our first signature dance, one of many that would go on to make people talk.

Our most controversial dance was "Topless Showgirls," performed in season 2. We had skimpy costumes with huge fans that we waved around in front of us as we moved across the dance floor. Abby kept stressing that the fans were meant to entice the audience, leaving them wanting more. Clearly, the sexual connotation of this dance was inappropriate given our ages, but her intention was to shock the judges, hoping it would secure a win. Abby was super passionate about this dance, but the moms agreed it was a little too edgy for our age group. This episode has since been banned; you cannot stream it or find it anywhere online. Our costume choice wasn't the real issue because we used the same costume about two weeks later in a dance called "Nip/Tuck." I'm guessing the problem was the overall effect of the costume, the choreography, and the theme.

"The Last Text" was a creepy, dramatic contemporary routine about the dangers of texting while driving. This routine was a favorite of season 3, and we were even asked to perform it on one of several appearances on *The View*. *The View* was an especially important opportunity for me because that's where I met Sherri Shepherd. She and I played a mother and daughter in a Lifetime movie several years after our first meeting. Another pivotal experience on *The View* occurred when I met Whoopi Goldberg. She showed us her closet, which was no ordinary closet. She had racks and racks of shoes, all of them so colorful and bright. I loved having this behind-the-scenes moment with her. She asked what I wanted to be when I grew up. When I proudly told her I wanted to be on Broadway, she responded, "We are waiting for you."

I get chills every time I think about that moment. Those positive words left a lasting impression on me. I still aspire to be on Broadway, and I've carried her encouragement with me as a light in the darkest times.

Although we had a seven-year agreement with Lifetime, our agreement with Abby's studio was separate. As the seasons went on, there were dancers who signed on to be a part of *Dance Moms* but were not necessarily part of the dance studio. Every once in a while, other students from the studio joined the team for a week or two, but the majority came from different dance studios around the country. The rest of us would have to adjust to dancing with each new member based on their personality and previous dance experience. Some girls were much easier to get along with than others, and some were easier to dance with than others.

Not to toot our own horn, but our core team—the OGs—danced like a *team*. We were in sync and knew how to support one another. Gianna would often say that she was proud of the fact we moved as one, breathed as one, and even blinked as one. We would put our all into a routine, and though we individually tried to draw Abby's attention to us in a positive way, we prioritized cohesiveness. This was not true for some of the newer dancers, who would try to stand out in our group dances. Some of them didn't blend in well because they did turns, jumps, or other tricks differently from the way we were taught. It made for a difficult dynamic and required adaptability from the rest of us.

The newer dancers did not necessarily sign the ALDC contract we were all beholden to, and they also had a different *Dance*

Moms agreement. Because of this distinction, we saw ourselves as real members of the dance studio, while the other dancers were just there to be on TV. Being on the show didn't necessarily equate to being the most talented dancer. Abby had several favorites who were not featured on *Dance Moms*, and, as we've already established, I certainly wasn't a favorite. I felt like she resented the fact that I was on the show and I was taking a space away from one of the dancers she would have preferred to feature. Abby liked winners, and I was not winning.

My standing as the dancer who'd been on the team the longest didn't win me any points either. When I spoke up about this, I would get tremendous backlash. People fumed that I was just expressing a bruised ego, but I never thought I was entitled to anything. I had been on the team for several seasons, working hard and patiently waiting for an opportunity to be featured or be seen as a future star. I had endured years of being forced into the left back corner (or LBC, as we affectionately called it) and relegated to the role of background dancer. I was not entitled; I was advocating for myself. I wanted my years of experience on and off the show to be taken into consideration—to mean something.

Unfortunately, to Abby, my years as a dancer on the elite team did not translate into much. The moms would often tell her not to put all her eggs in one basket. Imagine what the results could have been had she invested equitably in each dancer on her team, developing several successful and accomplished dancers instead of just one star.

Still, for someone who seemed to have no interest in supporting me, Abby was determined to command all my time and effort. She basically forced me to quit karate because she thought it worsened my "condition" of having bad feet. Though she never outright told me to quit, she would complain about me doing karate constantly. After the first season of *Dance Moms*, I gave it up because I was tired of hearing about it. Besides, dance meant more to me anyway. But she hardly needed to make these sorts of comments to control us; her expectations of our time were baked into the ALDC contracts us "core team" dancers had signed. We were prohibited from doing anything that might risk injury, including fun stuff like skiing, snowboarding, ice-skating, jumping on the trampoline, and roller skating. These limitations also extended to specific activities we couldn't do the night before a competition, like swim or work out, because they could make us sore the next day. In general, she hated when we had anything else going on besides dancing at her studio.

Despite the ways all these rules restricted the freedoms afforded most children, I hardly gave them a second thought. I was so dedicated to perfecting my craft that I was willing to do whatever it took to keep being an elite dancer.

With the show's success, I eventually struggled to balance in-person school attendance and my dance commitments. I attended traditional school through sixth grade, but for seventh and eighth grade, I switched to homeschooling. My parents didn't love the idea of my being homeschooled because they wanted me to have some sense of normalcy, but they saw how tired I was. I had even started falling asleep in class. I remember drifting off during math and being made to get up and do jumping jacks in front of the entire class. "That'll wake you up," my teacher said. I was so embarrassed. Homeschooling became my most sustainable option.

There was another reason why homeschooling was attractive to me: I wanted more time to train one-on-one with the teachers at the ALDC. I was determined to get better and to show how hard I was working so that Abby and the rest of the team would know I was dedicated to my craft and deserved my spot. Abby frequently held up Maddie—who was homeschooled—as an example of someone who put in the work, so I thought, *If that's what it takes to get Abby's attention in a positive way, I'll do it.*

My mom had quit her job early on, around season 2, so she ended up being my humanities teacher. I had a different tutor for math and science. We were still shooting primarily in Pittsburgh, so I would do school at home and then go to the studio to film. But in season 5, when we started going to LA more frequently, our schooling schedule shifted quite a bit, which resulted in doing school on set. Schooling on set was a little different from being traditionally homeschooled. Our sessions were not broken up by age or grade, so we typically sat together for our lessons in the mornings. Afterward, we'd go straight to dance. California has strict laws regarding minors in entertainment, and since we spent so much time in LA, we had to do three hours of school a day. But we could also bank hours if we had more time for schoolwork on certain days. We banked these hours when other dances outside of the group dance were practicing. I usually didn't have other dances outside of group dances, so I was always banking hours since I had extra time. This gave us more flexibility with our schedule. We could film when needed, travel, and attend appointments or see to any other obligations we had to fulfill.

Still, there were limitations. We were allowed to do school on set for a maximum of five hours per day, and we were required to do a minimum of one hour each day. Because of this, if one of the moms got into it with Abby and wanted to leave, they were sometimes forced to stay if their daughter hadn't finished school for the day. This didn't happen often, but I remember when it happened to me.

Imagine having the worst day ever: Abby yelled at you, and you're sad, upset, crying—you just want to leave. But as you get to your car, the producers and mic guy come over. They remove your mic and say, "You can't leave yet; you need to go to school." Not fun. I would literally just sit there for an hour in a random room and dissociate.

With the show came a lot of drama. Fans thought the drama was fake, but we weren't actors, and the things happening to us were very real. In fact, viewers would have likely been surprised to learn there was even more drama behind the scenes than what made it to air. I can think of at least one significant incident that happened to me while I was on the show. Our audience never learned about it, but they would have felt its effects; a lot changed after it happened.

At rehearsal one afternoon during filming for season 2, episode 10, Abby was fussing because we hadn't placed in the competition the week before. She went through pyramid; of course, I was at the bottom again, even though Abby was upset with the other girls as well. I was so excited to be given a solo that week, and if you watch the episode, you can see my joy radiating through my smile. Maddie, Chloé, and Paige had a trio, but Paige had to have surgery on her feet, so she wasn't sure she could participate. My mom discussed the situation with the other moms, and everyone agreed that I would be a good fit for the routine, so she came down to the studio and asked Abby if I could be Paige's swing—to do her part if she couldn't do it. While it was an honor to be given a solo, I was constantly being overlooked for trios, and this seemed like a perfect, natural opportunity to fill in.

Abby said that had been her plan all along and then got angry with my mom for asking. My mom was flabbergasted. If Abby was planning to do exactly what she was asking, why wouldn't she just say that? It could have been a win-win.

Things escalated quickly, and my mom got frustrated. "A mother looking out for her daughter trumps the word of a dance teacher," she finally said.[1]

This made Abby livid. She firmly believed that you abdicated all rights when you entered the studio. You had to obey everything she said, no exceptions or negotiations.

This part of the argument made it to air. But there was quite a bit more that didn't.

As they argued, Abby began talking about how I was the weak link and admitted that she'd never asked for me to be on the show. She went on and on about her vision for the ALDC and its competition team. She wanted a line of skinny girls who were the same height, with blond hair and blue eyes. She then proceeded to say that she didn't ask for "a Tootie," referring to Kim Fields's character on the hit 1980s show *The Facts of Life*. The subtext of the statement—that she didn't ask for a Black girl to be on her team of all-white dancers—hit hard. She later referred to this incident in her book, writing, "What were these producers thinking? Did any of them know anything about dance? What was I going to do with this team of misfit toys? Were they casting a new version of *The Facts of Life* TV show, or a competitive dance team? Some taller than others, some skinnier than others, some older than others, and some way better than others?"[2]

That Tootie comment was the last straw. My mom lost it.

I could see the look on Abby's face while my mom was going off on her. Abby turned beet red. She stalked toward me and yanked me by the arm, knocking me off balance. I was shocked that the situation had escalated to the point where Abby would put her hands on me.

My mom got in Abby's face and told her never to touch me again.

Abby was enraged. "No solo for you!" she yelled as she kicked me out of the studio.

It was clear to me that I had not been selected for the trio because I did not fit the look she was going for. And judging by Abby's other statements, I did not fit the look of the team, period.

The fact that production chose to leave out this part of the conflict felt like a cruel joke. Even the descriptions of this episode were appalling, saying only that I was "expelled."[3] What? We left! Walked out. Considering the gravity of what happened, the way the situation was edited for television felt insulting.

In the moment, though, this was taken quite seriously. Filming stopped immediately—something that never happened.

My mom was boiling hot by the time we got home and immediately told my father what had gone down. My parents had had enough of Abby's antics, and my mom wanted to pull me off the show. At that point, I didn't know if I was ever going back.

My parents called our lawyer to find out if we could legally get out of our production agreement. Meanwhile, I was just trying to wrap my ten-year-old head around everything that had happened. I remember sitting on the living room floor doing my homework while Mom paced back and forth, on and off phone calls. Though I hadn't been physically hurt, Mom was adamant no instructor should get away with aggressively touching a student the way Abby did when she threw me out.

We did not show up to set the next day. Our attorney was brought in to handle the situation. If we weren't able to get out of our contract with Lifetime, we needed assurance that safety measures would be in place to prevent this kind of thing from happening again.

You might not understand how I felt, but Abby not wanting me at the studio only made me want to be there even more. I *needed* to show her—show everyone—that I was good enough to be on the team and that no one was going to push me out. In hindsight, adult me recognizes that sometimes you don't have to prove a point. Often, "being right" is just not worth the mental and physical anguish that comes with the territory. However, leaving felt like quitting, and I was no quitter. If I left, I thought Abby would just replace me with a white kid. Moreover, I deserved to be there. I deserved to have an opportunity to dance with my team, to go to competitions, to travel the world and be on a nationally syndicated show. I would not let her get rid of me that easily.

As my family was going back and forth about what to do, we waited for some sort of apology from production or Abby, but for two days there was nothing of the kind. I kind of knew they weren't going to apologize because that would have meant admitting that Abby had done something wrong. By the time that weekend's competition rolled around, we still had no idea what was going to happen. Unsure what was expected—or legally required—of us, we packed our bags and headed to Miami.

Upon our arrival, we were met by the senior vice president of production, who came out to try to salvage the situation. He assured us that I would be safe on set, and though he could not make Abby apologize, she would be reprimanded. She was very upset, they said, and had been crying because she had never allowed herself to get to that point before. We were used to Abby's crocodile tears, so that alone was not enough to sway our hearts. He apologized for what had gone down and wanted us to know that they were doing something about it. Their solution was to hire a child therapist who would come to set to manage things between the girls and Abby.

Production also gave all of us girls brand-new iPads. The devices were new technology, and we all wanted them. At the time I thought production was just being nice, but once I got older, I realized the gifts had been a distraction from what happened. Honestly, it worked. We girls never talked much about the incident until after the show ended.

Everyone was on their best behavior that weekend. Even when I forgot my solo, Abby did not flip out. Nor did she have much to say when my mom asked the competition director to allow me to do my dance again. How could she? I had gone through so much beforehand and had to learn my solo literally overnight, so it was no wonder I blanked during that performance. Viewers may have seen this as proof that I was a weak dancer, but what I saw was a courageous girl who stood up to a giant. I think of my younger self as being so brave for competing after everything that had happened that week. I feel like I slayed a dragon.

As promised, production brought in a child advocate to work with us on the show and ensure the environment felt "safe." Of course, the concept of safety was relative. How safe could I ever really feel around Abby, given all that she'd voiced? Nevertheless, the girls and I were introduced to Stacy Kaiser, and she started coming in whenever things got really heated at the studio. She helped as much as she could, but we were constantly living on edge, anxious and worried about what we might do to set off Abby. It was like working next to a ticking time bomb.

Walking into the studio sometimes made me genuinely afraid. My heart would start racing as soon as we drove into the parking lot. This reaction didn't happen every day, but each day I did mentally prepare myself before walking into the studio. I'd hold my breath and hope she wasn't sitting at the intimidating front desk.

Abby's mood swings worked hard to negate the healthy environment Stacy was trying to create. A bad mood for her was a bad mood for everyone. When Stacy was there, things were good, and Abby was on her best behavior because she knew she was being watched. She would be nice and charming, trying to prove that she would never do anything to hurt us. Even then, I recognized that Abby was manipulative and engaged in gaslighting—though I didn't yet know what gaslighting was. If Stacy was around, Abby pretended like nothing bad ever happened. This would last long enough for us to get lulled into a false sense of security and safety before the other shoe dropped.

Though this volatility put a strain on our health, at the time we chalked it up to tough love. This was how our team operated. Things were a bit different for new dancers who came to the studio. They were more themselves, not indoctrinated into the studio culture, not so inclined to disassociate as a coping mechanism. So when people say their experiences at the ALDC were different from mine, I think it's because they were not an OG. They didn't know what it was like to grow up with Abby. And most of them didn't know what it was like to be Black around Abby either.

As time went on, rather than look forward to Stacy's visits, we began to dread them. Having held in all her aggression, Abby would usually slingshot in the other direction, and we would be treated worse once Stacy left.

Still, Stacy's presence validated our feelings. During my individual sessions with her, I tried to share openly about my experience, but it was difficult to articulate how I felt. I knew the treatment I received from Abby wasn't normal, but at the same time, it was all I knew. Add to that all the fans Abby had cheering her on, and I began to wonder if I was being overly sensitive. There was so much to unpack, but I was too young to do so.

Thankfully, Stacy did give me some useful tools to help me compartmentalize, stay focused, and not allow people to get inside my head and make me think untrue things about myself. These were skills that I could apply to both dance and everyday life. I couldn't help but wish, though, that rather than teaching us how to cope, the show had put their energy into teaching Abby how to be a better person. Making excuses for someone's poor behavior only enables them to continue their wrongdoing.

Many viewers think we never held Abby accountable, but that's not true. It's just that doing so had consequences. Standing up to her on behalf of your child got your mom labeled as crazy, mean, or a bad mother. The studio culture was not conducive to independent thinking or self-advocacy. Our parents' concerns were voiced both on and off camera. Moms complained to production, and production told the moms to complain to Abby, and then they would capture it on camera. It was a vicious cycle.

Abby's words were fierce, and I never wanted to be at the other end of them. I truly believed she thought by being tough on us, she was creating a Broadway-like experience that would prepare us for life as professional dancers in a cutthroat industry.

Television was also a cutthroat business. Despite the show's success and having a multi-season commitment, there was never any guarantee the show would continue. The network could decide at any time not to renew *Dance Moms.* At the close of each season, we had to wait for ratings to be assessed before the network would let us know the future of the show. It was an anxious sort of limbo, as our outside opportunities were restricted by the network, but we didn't have the security of knowing we'd be staying on with the network.

Things really hit the fan in season 3, when our moms decided to go on strike. They thought that if they banded together to protect one another, they would have more say in the filming conditions. At that time, Pennsylvania didn't have many child labor laws, so there was no end to the hours we spent on set. Our moms wanted us to be compensated fairly, to be fed before the crew, to have a designated area to rest and eat (there were no chairs and tables), and to have tutors who could help us with our homework.

The strike was depicted as a walkout on the show. Still, we were under contract, so we legally had to show up for work. Coming to set on strike meant sitting in the parking lot in our cars. Of course, that didn't make for an interesting storyline, so Abby came out to the cars to taunt us, saying that if we didn't come to dance, we would be replaced. All of us were scared, but Maddie was the most fearful and began to cry. It was hard to see her that way. I remember Abby yelling at us to get out of the cars and go to rehearsal. She was so angry with us for not defying our mothers.

Abby was allowed to bring in a team to replace us during this time. This was probably the beginning of Abby getting a taste for finding a new team. She also threatened to call the police on us for not coming inside. Who calls the police on their students for sitting in a parking lot? She had 911 on speed dial, which is funny in an ironic sort of way. Really, how difficult is it to type in three numbers? But I guess it must have been difficult considering how many times Abby called the police to the studio.

Eventually, after some negotiation, Lifetime came to an agreement with us, and we returned to work, jumping right back into our rigorous film schedule. Most of us were still physically attending school at this point, so we were grateful for the presence of the tutors our moms had pushed for. They helped keep us from falling behind in our schoolwork.

As time went on and *Dance Moms* gained more popularity, my schedule intensified. *Dance Moms* season 1 was only 13 episodes, but by season 2, we had filmed almost 30 episodes—more than double what we started with. In seasons 3 and 4, we were filming close to 40 episodes. Season 3 was particularly draining for us, and the moms ended up asking production for a reduction in episodes because it was just too much. Our seasons were broken up into halves—technically two seasons for the price of one—but since we had a contract for seven seasons, and producers wanted to fit in as many episodes as possible, they called these the A and B part of the season (season 3A and 3B, season 4A and 4B, and so on). We'd film forty to sixty hours a week for a forty-two-minute episode, forty out of the fifty-two weeks of the year. By the time season 7 wrapped, I'd filmed more than two hundred episodes in seven years. I had barely become a teenager, and *Dance Moms* had completely taken over my life.

I also began assisting with recreational classes at the dance studio, which was a lot of fun but one more thing added to my schedule. The busier my life got, the harder things became for my parents. The show, and everything it put me and Mom through, impacted my entire family. Dad held it down at home as much as possible, but my mother's obligations to the show meant she couldn't be there for her husband and sons. Fans of the show loved to say that I was the favorite child and that's why my mother chose to accompany me, but it wasn't like that at all. My parents never played favorites or implied in any way that they loved one child over another. They were simply committed to helping me pursue my dream.

I know people wonder why I came back and stayed. My family and I made that choice because production assured us that conditions would improve—and, to an extent, they did. If we felt like the work environment was hostile, we would contact our attorneys, the network, and production to address the situation. We'd drawn a line in the sand.

We stayed because I had earned my place on this TV show, and I deserved to be there. What's more, I was finally seeing the results I always wanted. One of my biggest accomplishments during season 4—that, unfortunately, wasn't shown on *Dance Moms*—was receiving that crown I had dreamed about as a kid. In 2014, I won my first national title. It was a big deal at the dance studio, and all the students at the studio were so happy for me. I was crying onstage as they crowned me.

Despite Abby's best efforts to keep me down, little Nia was getting everything she ever wanted. Abby wasn't going to be given the satisfaction of getting rid of the "Tootie."

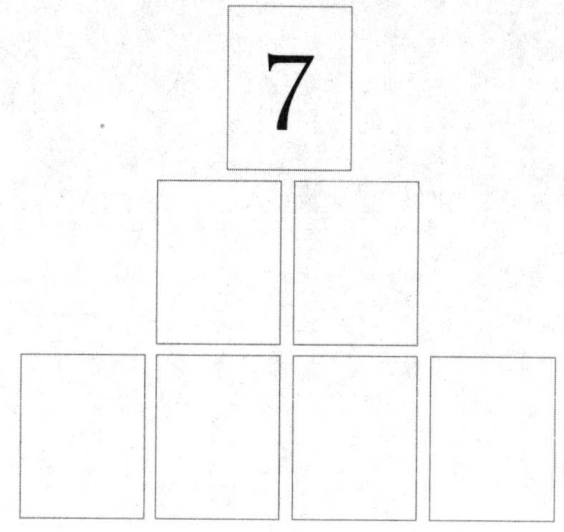

7

A New Passion

The cast of the show changed season by season. Some people left; some people joined. It was interesting to see what each member's breaking points were. Though we all went through the same things, we each handled certain scenarios differently. But soon, it started to feel like the original members were dropping like flies.

Paige and Brooke left after Abby and their mom, Kelly, got physical in season 4. I remember we girls were all so afraid because we'd never seen any kind of physical altercations on the show. When the argument escalated, my mom told all of us to step out of the room. Brooke started crying, which she never did, and Paige was in pure shock, just standing there with a blank stare. It was heartbreaking seeing my friends go through that. It was hard to even comfort them when something that traumatic happened. There's nothing you can say or do to help. Abby called the police as my mom helped to escort Kelly out. Brooke, Paige, and Kelly were off the show, and Kalani Hilliker and her mom, Kira, officially took their place. This was the first time we realized that despite our contracts, Abby had the power to get someone kicked off the show. I remember feeling like I couldn't trust anyone, particularly the moms. It was scary to see how far they would take things to push their kids ahead, often costing their kids' friendships. Since many of the moms didn't see me as a threat, I just kind of watched all this from the background.

Then, in season 5, Chloé left. Abby and Christi, Chloé's mom, had a falling-out, but that happened all the time on the show, so we were shocked to learn that they were really gone. The loss hit me especially hard because Chloé and I had always taken on the brunt of Abby's wrath, so she was an empathetic ear. The only two OGs that remained were Maddie and Kenzie. It dawned on me that I would now have to face Abby alone.

With Chloé gone, Abby used every opportunity to speak badly about her. This did not sit right with me and was hard to hear. I hated when someone would say anything bad about Chloé because she'd been such a core part of the show. Plus, she wasn't there to defend herself. Abby saying cruel things about her made me want to separate from Abby more.

The most painful part of Chloé's departure was that she cut me out of her life. At the time, I didn't understand what she was doing. I'd thought we were close, so I wanted some type of closure or a reason why she was distancing herself from me. Now that I'm older, I understand that she needed to separate from all things ALDC to protect her peace. To heal.

I've had to put similar boundaries in place with some castmates for my own well-being. That doesn't mean that those relationships can't be rekindled someday, but I've needed to separate myself from certain people to protect my mental health. Ultimately, Chloé's behavior taught me that boundaries are healthy, and when she finally returned to the show in season 7, I was profoundly happy.

Following Chloé's departure, JoJo Siwa, along with her mom, Jessalynn, joined the show. Jojo and I eventually had a good relationship, but the beginning was a bit rocky. She had a huge personality, unlike anything I had seen or been around before. Along with that personality came an enormous ego and not much empathy to what us fellow dancers were going through. One of the first comments she made to the girls was that she was there to replace Chloé. "The new and better blonde on the team," she called herself. She told us we were washed up and that she brought light to the team. Not only was I annoyed, but I was also surprised to hear a kid talk like this. No other dancer had ever come onto the team and been so unapologetically themselves. It was like she wasn't afraid of anyone, including Abby. JoJo's presence created an awkward vibe between the girls because, for the most part, we were pretty nice to anyone who came on the show. But JoJo got on everyone's nerves, including mine. It was like she was going out of her way to ruffle feathers and to get a reaction out of us. She shook up the team dynamic, for better or for worse.

Around this time, the *Dance Moms* cast had also begun spending more time in Los Angeles because Abby was looking to expand. Grandad, who was now eighty-two, was getting sicker, adding to the emotional turmoil I already felt. And to make matters worse, it seemed like JoJo and her mom used every opportunity to try to push me out of dances. Jess would constantly speak about how I wasn't needed and say that JoJo could take my place in group dances.

Jess had come to *Dance Moms*—and before that, its spinoff show, *Abby's Ultimate Dance Competition*—with a calculated plan to make JoJo a star.[1] Honestly, that's pretty smart—make the most of the opportunities that come to you, right? But what doesn't sit right with me is doing that at the expense of someone else. "I learned at a very young age that in the public eye, any attention is attention . . . whether it be good attention or just attention," JoJo told *People* magazine in 2024.[2] Jess and JoJo may have played up their behavior for the cameras, but what they were doing affected my real life. They knew I was struggling because of my grandfather, yet they showed me no mercy. The behavior may have been fake, but the impact on me was not.

With most of the original cast members and their moms gone, my mom and I became even more of a target for Abby, though Mom continued to stand up to her. Meanwhile, many of the new cast members were fans of Abby's, so they were not critical of her teaching methods and would not hold her accountable for her behavior. That's why, although I always knew Abby would rather have someone else on her team instead of me, I didn't feel like she was fully on a mission to get rid of me until the fifth season. She even prohibited me from doing any meet and greets for the studio during this season.

The tension worsened after Abby had success managing Kenzie's music career. She was trying to force her way into managing the rest of us. But there was no way I would let her do that for me—not after she tried to sabotage me during an audition in season 5. All of us from the studio were in LA at a casting call. I had been given a small part to recite in front of the casting director, and he was impressed by me. He said I had a great look and that he didn't have many notes to share regarding my performance. But Abby expressed her displeasure, saying, "She took the character in a different direction."[3] It completely deflated me. The director looked uncomfortable, and I was sad that she would try to ruin that moment for me. This woman had been my dance teacher since I was three years old. Why would she purposely try to sabotage any opportunity that came my way?

Naturally, this experience was heavy on my mind when she started talking about being my manager. *Absolutely not*, I thought.

Abby set up time for some of the girls to meet music producers at a recording studio, but I didn't even want to go. I wasn't going to let her manage me, so what would have been the point? It was only after Melissa begged my mom to have me go that I gave in to keep the peace. During our session, which took place after filming was completed for the day, the producers played an energetic, upbeat pop song for us. I expressed that I liked the beat and that it reminded me of something Beyoncé would sing to. Then Abby announced that Kendall would be recording to that song. I was disappointed, but there were other tracks to consider. Next, they played a song that sounded deep and slow, like the hymn to a gospel record. Abby looked over at me and said, "Nia, this one is for you. I was thinking you could do gospel." She expressed to me that I needed to sing "soulful" music. Why did she feel that I had to sing gospel? I love gospel music, don't get me wrong, but at twelve or thirteen years old, that wasn't my passion. It was clear to me she thought I should do gospel because I was Black.

Abby may have had the power to stereotype me when it came to dance, but I wasn't about to let her do that with music—or anything else, for that matter.

At least one thing came out of Abby pushing to be my manager: I ended up working with Aubrey O'Day. I met Aubrey during the summer before we filmed season 5. Abby sometimes held master classes, events where we would serve as demonstrators or assistants and members of the public could come dance with us. I met Aubrey and her goddaughter at one of those master classes. Aubrey is best known for her work as a singer with the pop group Danity Kane. Since then, she has gone on to a solo singing career, done some modeling, and performed on Broadway. She has also been on shows like *Celebrity Apprentice* and *Famously Single*. Everyone was stoked to see her in attendance.

Aubrey had asked Abby who the best singer in the group was,

and Abby said me. But when Aubrey asked why I didn't have an album, Abby just shrugged. My mom ended up meeting her, and they sat together and talked. Aubrey questioned my mom about why I hadn't pursued music, and Mom explained that she didn't know anyone in the music industry and had no idea how to get started. Aubrey said she would help. It was as simple as that. My mom couldn't believe it.

I was so excited. At the beginning of each season, the moms met with the producers to talk about anything that we wanted to have them follow or highlight, and my mom mentioned Aubrey seeking me out and wanting to help me pursue music. The producers loved this and wanted to showcase the story. Cameras would follow me around and capture my music journey. I was nervous but thrilled about this new opportunity outside of the show. I couldn't wait to get started.

Fast-forward to one day after pyramid. Abby was in a raging mood because my mom had called her out. After the moms left the studio to sit in the waiting area, we dancers came in to stretch and get ready to start learning our piece for the week, as we normally did. Since we were in LA, the moms were stationed in the waiting area of the building with a TV, allowing them to see but not hear what was happening. Abby was sitting in her chair, going on about one thing or another. Then all of a sudden, she took out her cell phone and made a call. She put the phone on speaker while I continued stretching with the other girls, not paying much attention to her. Once the call connected and I heard the voice on the other end of the line, however, I froze.

It was Aubrey. Abby told her that she'd heard we were working together. As she said this, she looked right at me. She went on to tell Aubrey that my mom wasn't supposed to contact her behind

Abby's back, that *she* was my manager, and that she was hurt by my mother using one of her contacts to make an underhanded deal. She then offered Aubrey $10,000 not to work with me.

I was a pretty tough kid to break, but Abby's cruel bribe made me crumble. I was crushed. Literally the one good thing I'd had going for me was just ruined. I remember that awful, gut-wrenching feeling of my heart sinking to my stomach. It was like someone had ripped out my insides and thrown them on the ground.

A lot of this got edited out of the episode when it aired. The network made it seem like the girls weren't in the room and the moms were, and they also cut out the part where Abby bribed Aubrey. They didn't even show me running out of the room, crying and looking for my mom. Rather than show the incident in its entirety, the episode seemed to protect Abby and any sense of "likability" she had with the audience. Usually when a kid cried, the producers were all over it, but since this was so malicious and vindictive, they had to protect their interests. This was the kind of thing that could've gotten the show canceled—or at least in really hot water.

One of the hardest things to accept was that no one else seemed to care. None of my teammates nor their mothers even bothered to check on me after this. They'd all witnessed the worst day of my life firsthand, and no one did anything about it. Sometimes other moms would comfort the girls or speak words of encouragement to make them feel better when they were troubled. I got none of that. Instead, some of the other moms told us we'd brought the situation on ourselves and that we should have taken Abby up on her offer to manage me. That's when it sank in that I was alone in this *Dance Moms* world. No one was coming to save me—well, no one except my mom. It was now us against the world.

I figured there was no way Aubrey would want to work with me after this, so you can imagine my surprise when she contacted us to say how horrible Abby's actions had been. Rather than deter her, it made Aubrey want to work with me even more. Relief rushed over me in waves. I was so grateful that Aubrey still wanted to take a chance on me.

I still don't know why Aubrey was so kind to me. Most people would have been scared away by Abby, but she wasn't. She saw right through my coach's BS.

Aubrey took me to meet a music producer by the name of R8dio, who had worked with artists like Solange, Beyoncé, and Will Smith. He was amazing to work with and was enthusiastic about the music I was interested in making. R8dio took me under his wing and made me feel like a superstar. It was incredible to have genuine support from such well-established professionals in the industry. My music team made me feel validated and seen because they recognized what I had to offer.

R8dio brought in a songwriter, Kamilah, for me to collaborate with. This was my first time helping to write song lyrics. When I was asked by R8dio and the songwriter what kind of song I wanted to make, I said I wanted something fun that I could hear on the radio. I imagined an R & B song with meaning behind it, something that made people feel empowered. I was adamant that it needed to be encouraging. Almost like a hype song, especially for those going through tough times.

I told them I would love to incorporate a saying my mom and Nana would always tell me: "Star in your own life." Since I was consistently at the bottom of the pyramid, fading into the background, this saying helped remind me that no one else got to be the lead in my story. Only *I* got that privilege.

The process was so cool. I watched in awe while R8dio and the writer came up with beats and melodies. I love how they involved me from start to finish. They would ask me if I liked the lyrics or how certain instruments sounded. They even encouraged me to add my own lyrics. I chimed in with ideas here and there. Kamilah did the background vocals and also laid down the tracks. Having her voice to follow helped me stay on beat while recording. Before I knew it, I had my debut single, "Star in Your Own Life."

The recording studio is vastly different from a dance studio. It's quiet, much smaller, and way less distracting. In many ways it brought me peace in an otherwise-chaotic environment. I loved going there even though I was super nervous about singing. I'd sung in front of audiences before, but this was a room full of music legends, experts who'd worked with stellar acts in the business, and I was afraid I'd disappoint them—in front of the cameras, no less. Despite my fears, the song turned out well. We ended up also making a remix, which had even more energy.

After we released "Star in Your Own Life," we began working on the music video. Aubrey connected me to Mikey Minden, the creative director for the Pussycat Dolls. I had no idea I'd be doing a video, much less having creative input on it. The feeling was priceless! Mikey brought in an amazing choreographer, Kenya Clay, and I had rehearsals, fittings, and hair and nail appointments all leading up to the shoot.

I loved Mikey's vision. He saw me and treated me like a star, while making sure everything ran smoothly and professionally. He got the best of the best to jump on this project, even going so far as to bring in a cast of dancers for A-list artists, an incredible stylist, and a top glam team. My hair was done up by the same guy who styled Katy Perry's hair; my makeup was applied by

Janet Jackson's makeup artist. I was in awe of everyone I got to work with.

The day of the shoot, everything revolved around me. It felt good—and weird—being front and center. It was the happiest I'd felt in a long time. For once I got to feel important. I mean, I always knew I was important, but I didn't really *feel* it until that day.

The video was creative and inclusive. We even had two guys vogueing, a concept I loved because it allowed me to showcase my support of the LGBTQIA+ community. Mikey reminded me that queer people felt underrepresented or like they weren't important or that no one cared about them. I had experienced those same feelings often in my life, and I wanted to show my support and celebrate our magic.

Mikey opened my eyes to so much in a short span of time. He not only helped my career but also made sure I understood how the music business worked and how to be professional. The guidance I received was so much better than anything I'd experienced before.

My mom was beside herself. She was so happy and told me that this was all she had ever wanted for me. I was glad that she finally felt like she could help me achieve that goal. She knew how patient I'd been and how grateful I was for the opportunity.

The whole process was an all-around great time, and I wanted to do it again. Soon after, I released my second song, "Slay." It's arguably the best song I've ever made, and I was proud to have contributed a bulk of the lyrics. "Slay" is my most popular song to date and has been used in commercials and as background music for *The View* and *The Real Housewives of Beverly Hills*, as well as on the Disney Channel.

For "Slay" I worked with Coco Jones, an amazing R & B singer,

Grammy Award winner, and Disney star. She also starred in *Bel-Air*, the revamp of *The Fresh Prince of Bel-Air*. I was so excited because I had grown up watching her on the Disney Channel. I could hardly believe I was making a song with someone I looked up to so much. And boy, can she sing! She really made the song what it is; her voice tied everything together.

I realized how much I loved being a part of the writing process. It felt natural to have this new outlet, a new medium to tell stories and to make people feel something. When I started writing music, I think it made me like writing more in general. I was told to keep a journal, or at least notes of my thoughts, because it would come in handy for my music. I could pull from different experiences I've lived and incorporate my emotions and feelings into the lyrics. My journals, Notes app, and Google Docs are full of miscellaneous thoughts that could someday be fodder for my next song.

Working with Mikey Minden really helped to boost my self-esteem. Mikey was intentional about the clothes he put me in. He chose items that showcased my beauty, something I hadn't seen in myself for a long time. I finally felt comfortable in my own skin, wearing outfits that fit me well and looked great. They were cute but edgy and cool. Being able to see myself in this light helped me begin to like the way I looked. Everyone kept telling me I looked great, but for the first time I actually believed it.

I don't know if Aubrey or Mikey understand how much their support means to me. How being around people who wanted to help me, who saw something in me, kept me going. I've met some extraordinary people in my journey who have guided me and become mentors. I never would have experienced any of this without those two.

I'm glad my mom made the connection with Aubrey and that Aubrey took a chance on me. That she didn't allow Abby's unconscionable behavior to pull her in a different direction. She went out of her way to help me when she didn't have to, and she will always hold a special place in my heart.

The Turning Point

By about midway through season 5, my grandfather, who had always been one of my biggest supporters, had become quite sick with dementia and was now in hospice care. We didn't know if he would survive long enough for me to compete that week and return home. For weeks we'd been traveling back and forth to LA, and I was glad that we'd be in Pittsburgh for the coming weekdays so I could visit him.

I was nervous to leave for that weekend's competition, and I rushed home after we'd finished Saturday night so I could go see him first thing Sunday morning. His condition weighed heavily on my mind and that of the entire dance studio. The others at the ALDC were familiar with him from the many times he had dropped me off for dance over the years.

But when I woke up on Sunday, I learned that he had passed away. I was devastated. I didn't even get to say goodbye.

This was the biggest loss I had experienced. I was just thirteen when he died. Episode 4 of season 5 was dedicated to him. Grandad had always loved to watch me on TV. He'd thought it was the coolest thing. This was a beautiful gesture from the producers for a man who was such a special part of my life. Having the ability to write about him now, to give him the honor and respect he deserves, means so much to me.

Every once in a while I see people comment on social media about my racial identity, stating that since my grandfather was a white man, that makes me biracial. I know he would have found that hilarious. He was 100 percent Black, just as I am. Now that I look back on it, though, I can see how his complexion might have caused his ethnicity to come into question. He told me that when he was younger, people used to call him "Red" because of his fair skin and red hair. So I understand the confusion.

Although my grandfather passed away about ten years ago now, I still miss him dearly. My granddad and I had a special bond, and the memories I made with him will stay with me forever.

Since we spent so much time in LA, my mom and I would explore the city whenever we had free time. We also met a lot of people and started making friendships outside of the show. We'd go to the movies, shopping, out to dinner, museums—anything that brought us joy and took us out of the toxic ALDC environment, even if only for a few hours, especially since things had changed drastically at the studio.

By the conclusion of season 5, Abby had finally opened her studio location in LA. The team consisted of Kendall, Maddie, Kenzie, Kalani, JoJo, Brynn Rumfallo, and me. Although we'd been back and forth to LA for about a year doing competitions and other events, we were now working out of Abby's new studio instead of other dance studios around town, solidifying our team's "LA dynamic."

I received fewer solos now, but I was starting to see a silver lining. Fewer solos meant I had a little more time for myself. When we made the commitment to move to LA for *Dance Moms*, my mom and I were very clear that I wasn't coming just to dance at Abby's studio—I was going to start acting and making music too. I was tired of waiting for opportunities to be given to me and realized that if I wanted to make something happen, I was going to have to do it myself. So, on our days off, I would attend voice lessons, and in the evenings after filming, I would take acting classes. I went to auditions, events, and dance classes. I was out and about, trying to meet as many people as possible.

In addition to being given fewer solos, I was no longer participating in ALDC-led master classes or anything else the team was doing. I wasn't bothered by it because I was fed up with these ALDC events, anyway. When I went to them, I would always sell the fewest autographed photos out of all the girls, which took a toll on my ego. And it hurt when fans would bring gifts for the other girls and not me. At this point, I'd been essentially replaced by Kalani. "Everyone's replaceable," Abby had said more than once, and I was now getting a taste of that firsthand. I soon found that my removal from these events was a blessing. My lack of participation helped to protect my peace.

At this point, Abby was making the girls wear her branded clothes, not just on pyramid days but everywhere. Since Abby didn't invite me to her events anymore, I refused to wear ALDC dance attire and focused instead on how I could be my best self. When I'd show up in regular clothes, not matching the other girls, she'd say things like, "Wouldn't it be nice if all the girls showed up looking presentable?" Nothing she could say to me now was any worse than anything she'd already said to me over the years, though, so I brushed off these comments.

Though dancers had come and gone since season 3, by season 5 our team was like a revolving door. Every week someone different would join, and we'd have no idea if they were going to stay or for how long. People always thought they could come onto the show to be the next Maddie or to beat her in competition. But Abby was never going to let that happen; I knew that from personal experience. After I came close to beating Maddie—losing by only a tenth of a point—I didn't get a solo again for a long time. Abby would give the new dancers solos, but they were never as good as Maddie's and didn't stand a chance against hers. Once new team members saw a glimpse of how it all operated, they left.

It was unsettling watching new people join the team who had not been training with Abby but got solos or featured parts in dances anyway. I'd waited my turn while other dancers on the original team were showcased, and when they left, I'd thought I would get my chance. It did not work out that way.

Getting solos week after week helps dancers improve their technique and gain confidence. Technique matters, but it is not the end-all, be-all of what makes a strong dancer. Dance should make people feel something. It should be memorable. I knew I was a great performer, and I was eager to show that off. So of course I was bothered by newcomers getting promoted on arrival. I couldn't fathom why people thought I should feel any different. As much as some viewers were annoyed with my perceived entitlement, I was frustrated they thought I should remain a background dancer to everyone else.

I could no longer deny the effects that being at the ALDC had on me, and I wanted no part of it. Hearing the things the other mothers said to my mom—"Oh, your kid's bad" or "My girl can outdance your girl anytime"—took a toll. The newer cast members, it seemed, were willing to do and say whatever they felt necessary to get the most airtime, but my mom and I weren't like that. Nothing was more important than our integrity.

For so long, dance had been everything to me. No matter how hard it got, I knew I was in it for a reason. That my loyalty, hard work, training, and constant drive to be better would work out for me in the long run. But as the show neared the end of its run, I found myself questioning more and more why I was doing this in the first place. Before the cameras, before the fame, I was just a girl who wanted to dance. Now I yearned for new guidance to push me along in my professional endeavors.

There was no longer a social component to the team for me or that sense I'd initially had of fitting in. When I had a video premiere party in Pittsburgh that was filmed for the show, my team did not come out to support me. That hurt. Even the Candy Apples—our rival team—and Cathy, their coach, had shown up. It was embarrassing. So many of the girls were under Abby's thumb. They would go on and on talking about me, making snide comments regarding my music, my videos, my song lyrics, the outfits, the dancers. Some of them were "surprised" and "taken aback" that I had gay people in my music video. A few of the moms commented that my look was too mature. I thought, *Are these people for real?* These were the same women who'd supported nine-year-olds wearing skimpy and inappropriate outfits and dancing mature routines. Maddie literally did the "Chandelier" music video in a nude leotard at like eleven years old! But my outfits were too revealing and mature? The double standards drove me crazy.

Rather than attempt to prove myself as I'd done in the past, I ignored the other girls and moms, which only pushed them to further distance themselves from me. I would show up, do what I had to do to get through the day, then go home, treating the show like my job and nothing more. Abby was annoyed when I was off shooting my music videos, so she chose not to include me in several of the group dances. Still, I was required to go to rehearsal and put in the same hours as everyone else.

Though I enjoyed doing music, my time in LA brought a roller coaster of emotions. I'd go from being happy while working on new music and recording in the studio to feeling anxious and afraid as I entered our dance studio. I couldn't get Abby's voice offering Aubrey money out of my mind. I never knew what she was going to say or do, and it felt like I was constantly walking on eggshells. No matter how hard I tried to stay out of her way, I somehow managed to catch her wrath. I quickly learned that being the center of attention came with extreme bouts of joy and pain. But the sense of joy that music gave me was something I hadn't felt in a long time.

Midway through the season, I was excited to head to Australia. *Dance Moms* was invited to perform at the Astra Awards, an Australian slate of awards ceremonies that include the Astra Creative Arts Awards, the Astra Film Awards, and the Astra TV Awards. Though we were invited to perform for the show, Abby used this opportunity to tack on an ALDC tour—for everyone but me and JoJo. Since things had gotten so bad for me at the studio, my mom and I had decided not to renew my contract with the ALDC. Consequently, we were ostracized by Abby and the moms and were excluded from all activities.

Abby wanted to show my mom and me that she could use her influence to get us blackballed. She barred us from anything she put on, which turned out to be a blessing in disguise because the previous master classes she held overseas became part of the reason she got into trouble and would later wind up in prison. I truly dodged a bullet and cannot be more thankful I wasn't involved in any of that.

Because I was still a part of the elite competition team on *Dance Moms*, I went with the others to Australia, but I wasn't doing anything with Abby outside of the show—not ALDC competitions, not meet and greets, not master classes, none of it. Mom and I spent most of our time together or with JoJo and her mom, who were also not on good terms with Abby. Producers thought it would be a good idea for the four of us to get to know one another better, and this trip allowed for a genuine connection. We went sightseeing and traveled to restaurants as a small group.

While Abby and her squad did their thing, I pursued my own interests. I had an amazing opportunity to perform my single while there, which ended up being one of my absolute favorite moments from the show. I had announced and prepared for this performance only a couple of days prior and was amazed that more than one thousand people showed up to watch me. I don't think my song was even out yet, because *Dance Moms* didn't air until months later. The show was in Melbourne at Federation Square. Mikey Minden choreographed and directed my performance. Since JoJo was often left out of ALDC things, I invited her to be a part of it too. She came onstage and made an appearance in my dance break section.

The crowd was so huge and loud that day. They were cheering and going wild. They even formed their own runway during the show for people to strut down. It was so fun and energetic. My song was doing exactly what it was meant to do—make people happy and confident. We had an awesome time, even though most of the team did not show up. Melissa and Jill did eventually come, but they didn't stay long. I shouldn't have been surprised, since no one from the studio had come to the video release party. Still, the experience of performing on that stage will stay with me always because people were finally affirming my talent. They didn't see me as a weak link. They had high expectations for me, and I rose to the occasion.

Despite a tough start to the season, with losing my granddad and being isolated by a lot of the team, I felt like this was a turning point for me.

That trip to Australia put so much into perspective. I saw what I was able to do in just a couple of days. Imagine what I could do in a lifetime. I was stepping into a new era for myself. That experience showed me that I didn't need Abby to succeed. I could reach the top of the pyramid without her and the other ALDC girls. I could make a name for myself. This realization drove me to want to continue my passion for music and see where it could take me. I may not have been winning dance competitions, but I had support from fans. For me, that was the biggest win.

Hanging with the OGs

In telling my story, I don't want to come across as if I'm throwing any of the girls under the bus. I am only speaking about my experience, my perspective. As with any sisterhood, friendship, or relationship, there will always be ups and downs. At the end of it all, the strength of a relationship is about how you overcome those hardships and move past them. In some cases, you may come out even stronger than you were in the beginning.

That's how it was with me and the OG cast—Maddie, Kenzie, Paige, Chloé, and Brooke. We always had respect for one another and never bad-mouthed one another publicly or aired out anyone's dirty laundry. Sure, there were moments when we'd each be closer to one person over the other, but we all had a special bond due to our shared experience on a national TV show and dealing with Abby.

Most of us spent more than a decade with one another, starting when some of us were as young as three years old through to our teenage years. Sometimes we did fight, but there was a lot of love among us. Though not all future cast members would go on to be respectful of the other dancers when they reflected on their experiences, the OG cast was never unkind or malicious. I can wholeheartedly say those girls are amazing, truly some of the most down-to-earth and kind people I know.

As for some of the things that went down between us in the past: We were kids. Kids make mistakes and poor decisions. I know I did. Our brains weren't fully formed yet. Most of our brains still aren't fully developed yet because most of us are only in our early twenties. I blame a lot of the conflicts that happened on Abby and the mothers, who were the adults and could have done better.

Outside of the show, we were a bunch of little girls who loved having fun with one another. We had playdates, shared birthdays, hosted sleepovers, and attended movie nights. I remember going over to Maddie and Kenzie's house, way before the show started, and jumping on their big trampoline in their backyard. I rode to dance competitions with Chloé in her mom's minivan. We had fun on and off the show. The moms did a good job of making sure we still had opportunities to be kids even though we were working at such a young age.

One fun moment I'll never forget is when we went to see Justin Bieber. We all were such huge fans of his. We met up at Chloé's house and traveled to the stadium in a limo. What we didn't know then was that we would actually have the chance to meet him at the Teen Choice Awards a year later. It was like a full-circle moment. The *Dance Moms* girls did, in fact, have a picture taken with Justin Bieber on the red carpet. It was the first award show we ever attended but also the first time *Dance Moms* was nominated for a major award. I remember this moment well because we were almost in tears when we saw him. He was taking paparazzi pictures, and we were at the end of the red carpet, dying to meet him. The photographers were shouting for us to stand back, but Justin saw us and called us over to him. I'm surprised none of us got hurt stumbling over each other to get to him! Somehow I managed to stand right next to him. Best moment of my childhood.

Having spent so much time together, we got to learn one another's interests. All the girls knew about my love of dogs.

I would read dog books all the time, and I even had books that broke down dogs by the size, breed, and habits. I loved receiving anything dog-related as presents. When I was ten, I really wanted a dog. I often asked my parents to take me to the pet shop so that I could play with the puppies. After a while, they stopped taking me because I would cry hysterically each time I had to leave without one.

After much begging and pleading, they finally acquiesced and took me back to the pet shop sometime around my eleventh birthday. There, I found my dream dog, this tiny teacup Yorkie that I named Henry. Even though I didn't own him, for some reason, I named him, and I felt like he was mine.

For my birthday, Chloé and I had a joint party at her house. All our dance and school friends were invited. That morning, I asked my mom if we could go visit Henry before the party.

"He isn't there anymore, sweetie. He found a home," she said.

I was crushed, but my mom told me not to be upset because I had a fun party to look forward to. Soon after I arrived, Paige rushed up to me and handed me a large gift bag. "Nia, you have to open this one right now!" she said.

All the girls came over to watch me open the bag. Inside was Henry! I wept for joy. All the girls had pitched in to get me this dog for my birthday, and it was one of my most special, wholesome moments with them.

Another thing we loved to do was make music videos on Video Star, an app that had all these special effects that you could use. We'd put on makeup, dress up, and dance as silly as possible for our self-made videos.

When we traveled, we would often get together in one of the girls' rooms the night before the competition, while the moms went to dinner. Since Brooke was the oldest, she would be in charge of us. We would do what we called "ugly dance-offs" and play "Wizard of Oz," which was kind of like playing house, but instead of acting the role of a family member, we'd pick roles we wanted to play from the Broadway show. We'd occasionally get mani-pedis together but not often because we weren't allowed any colored nail polish—only nude or clear nails, per Abby's orders.

As we got older and spent more time in LA, we'd go out to dinner, the movies, or shopping. We stayed right across the street from the Grove, a popular mall in LA, which made for a perfect hangout spot. We went to Disneyland together, or to Duff's CakeMix to decorate cakes, or to cool lookout spots.

When we hung out socially, there was no competition—no Abby to create tension between us. We could just be kids. But things tended to look a little different in the ALDC studio or at ALDC events.

As I got older, I started to understand why I kept getting left out. The girls weren't intentionally excluding me or trying to hurt my feelings—they just didn't think of me. I am not saying that the girls were racist, but I do think they naturally gravitated toward each other because they shared a cultural identity. I was the only Black kid, the one who didn't look like the others. The oddball that stood out. The message Abby ingrained in us that I wasn't a good dancer created even more of a barrier. Sometimes I sensed that the girls thought they were better than me, and it tainted our interactions.

Just as I felt like a backup dancer in Abby's eyes, I started to feel like a backup friend. I wasn't automatically included in get-togethers, sleepovers, and concerts, and I noticed that invitations were extended only when someone else wasn't available or perhaps when two of the girls were getting on each other's nerves. I wasn't the first-choice friend for anyone except Kenzie, and I couldn't understand why. I now believe that racial differences made it difficult for the other girls to fully understand me. Sometimes this showed up in little ways, like when they wanted to go swimming and I had to tell them I couldn't get my hair wet and would need to sit out.

On a larger scale, I was always aware of the societal double standard that said a "fun antic" for them as white girls was something I could get in trouble for as a Black girl. They could just be kids and make mistakes and get a slap on the wrist, but I knew my punishment for the same thing would be worse. I had to be more reserved or guarded. I always had to think twice before doing something and did not have the luxury of being a carefree child.

Geography was an issue too. If I was left out and asked why, they'd often say it was because I didn't live in their area. Which was true, but the logic had a flaw: Chloé usually *was* invited, and we were neighbors. At the end of the day, however, I do think that my exclusion was less about me and more about all these other factors. Some of the girls had more dances together, so they formed tighter friendships that way—like Paige, Chloé, and Maddie, who were often cast in trio dances. But as a child, I didn't see things this clearly or objectively. All I saw was my friends showing up together at the dance studio, filing out of one car in matching outfits. I'd then spend rehearsal listening to them talk about the fun evening they'd just had, and all their reasons as to why I hadn't gotten an invite fell flat.

These dynamics evolved over time, just as the show did. By season 4, Paige and I got close. We had a lot of fun together until she and Brooke left the show, after which Chloé and I bonded over

Abby's unfair treatment of us. In the later seasons, with the roster constantly changing and girls coming in and out, oftentimes only for certain performances, it was hard to get close to anyone. And my continuous spot at the bottom of the pyramid wasn't making me popular among new dancers.

Maddie had always been Abby's favorite, which meant a lot of the girls wanted to be close to her. When we became adolescents, the friendships turned into cliques, and that hurt. I think that if Abby had said I was a good dancer, the girls would have wanted to get closer to me as well.

Once Chloé left, I really felt alone. At times, I felt like I was fighting for my life, without a single friend to hang out with.

I don't hold animosity toward the girls. It wasn't their fault how things went down. Every one of us has been through so much. Still, the years of social isolation were extremely painful to go through. But I'm grateful for the hard lesson they taught me: that I needed to love myself and be my own biggest fan. I worked to develop the mindset that if someone didn't invite me somewhere, it was their loss. I also accepted that sometimes, others' behavior truly has nothing to do with me.

Though the girls and I were on the same team, we were also competing against one another, and this naturally bred a more hostile environment. Everyone can't be number one—or in this case, at the top of Abby's pyramid. People still place my accomplishments against that of my castmates all these years later. But I've learned there is no race to success. I am not gauging the value of my achievements based on anyone else's. My teammates all have so much to offer the world. Even though people pitted us against one another when we were younger, I think today we all are happy for each other's wins.

I've kept great relationships with my OG girls. I have such amazing memories with them, even post–*Dance Moms*, like Maddie doing my makeup for prom and piercing the second holes in my ears for my eighteenth birthday. Chloé and I have been able to spend so much time together, going to our favorite restaurants and getting to be teenagers and college students together. I'll never forget her treating my mother and me to high tea at the Plaza Hotel for her birthday and Mother's Day. I love celebrating Kenzie's birthday each year, and I was thrilled to go to her concert when she went on tour. I cherish the impromptu get-togethers with Paige and Brooke when I'm home in Pittsburgh. Running into the Hyland sisters and their brother, Josh, at a bar in Lawrenceville after Brooke got engaged was such a surreal and special moment.

After everything we went through, we've all made it out as well-adjusted adults. We may go years without talking to one another because life gets in the way, but something always happens to push us together again, and we connect like no time has passed. The shared understanding, love, and respect us OG dancers have for one another is beautiful. Even our moms have been cordial and kept in touch. After all, they went through just as much as we did.

I'm thankful for the healthy friendships I have created and maintained since the show, and I value each and every one of them long after it's ended.

Token Black Dancer

Being the only Black girl on the team for most of *Dance Moms* was challenging. My mom and I dealt with microaggressions and racism daily. It felt like the producers and Abby needled Mom in a lot of different ways to try to bait her into behaving like the trope of the angry Black woman, but my mom wouldn't succumb to their agenda. She wasn't interested in playing a character—she just wanted to be herself. My mom was also a principal for the first two seasons of the show, so she had to hold her standards even higher, not only for the sake of herself and other Black people, but also for her students, parents, and faculty. She couldn't just do or say whatever she wanted.

My mom and I felt some things that happened on the show were inappropriate and racist, but we didn't have much power to stand up to it. We tried our best to set a good example so we wouldn't be labeled as angry, but that itself was frustrating since it's only human to get emotional. I hated the double standard, and it led to me feeling uncomfortable crying or showing any strong emotions. Other girls and their moms could do whatever, say whatever. They could make mistakes, swear, and act crazy without people labeling them as aggressive troublemakers. The pressure to rise above this was a lot for a nine-year-old, but that's part of life for a Black woman. Black girls are often forced to grow up faster and have to be more aware of the things they do and say, even if they're not on TV.

A lot of areas of Pittsburgh are predominately white, especially the areas some of my castmates were from, and I encountered many microaggressions. I didn't always know how to respond—I couldn't, really, because I was a child. If I developed an attitude, I'd get in trouble with Abby, and my mom would remind me that acting out would make me look bad. I couldn't jeopardize my career by talking back. I realized that between the two of us, only my coach got to act like a child.

Growing up Black already comes with "the talk" at a young age about how the world works. Black kids learn quickly that teachers might think they are not as smart as other children because they're Black. Or that they need to act a specific way if put in a situation with a white person of authority, like a police officer—or a dance teacher.

I definitely sensed Abby had race-based perceptions of me, assuming I was inferior. She claimed my mom didn't love me because she worked and pretended my parents couldn't afford to pay her, which was untrue. But many viewers believed her when she said those things. It seemed clear to me that she thought Black people were beneath white people, and I feel she tried to use me as an example to bolster that belief. This only added to my need to prove myself.

Mom and I needed to temper our responses as a form of protection. I'm glad my mom reminded me not to talk back or to let someone take me out of character. At the time it was annoying having my mom be so cautious about what I said and did, but she really did protect me. Despite never having been on TV before, she knew just what our situation called for. "As long as you stay true to yourself, you won't do anything you regret," she told me repeatedly. This is hard to keep in mind in the heat of the moment; it's much easier to lash out and say something impulsive. But in the long run, our grounded mindset helped my mom and me tackle every obstacle that came with being on the show.

One of my most well-known solos from *Dance Moms* was "They Call Me Laquifa," a comedic jazz dance I performed in season 1. The song was by the artist Shangela, a well-known drag queen whom I met later on in the season. Now, this solo stirred the pot because of the way Abby presented it. She put me in a cheetah-print costume and an Afro wig. My mom was fuming because it felt like Abby was mocking Black people. Was this image Abby's idea of the Black experience? Abby even asked my mom if she had an Afro wig. My mom jokingly replied, "Let me just pull it out of my purse."[1]

Abby frequently came across to my mom and me as thinking she knew everything—even about being Black. Whenever Abby said something that suggested she knew more about being Black than we did, my mom would get irritated and have to correct her.

But trying to convey the complexities of race on national television is difficult. Serious matters were rarely discussed on *Dance Moms*, and if they were, they were usually reduced to an argument that came across as silly or controversial.

I'm not saying that Black people don't wear Afros. There is nothing wrong with wearing an Afro! They're part of Black culture. But the way Abby wanted me to wear it felt mocking—a tool for amusement and not celebration. When my mom voiced her dissatisfaction, Abby responded that I'd better get used to it; there would be plenty more routines like this in my future since I was Black.[2] That was one of the first times viewers saw a glimpse of

Abby's racism on the show. Later she would admit to dance legend Debbie Allen that though she "didn't see color," she would often typecast Black dancers by choosing roles for them where race was important.[3]

But again, I was so young. I was just excited to have a solo, and I was fixated on my costume because it came with a gold crop top that was covered in rhinestones. I wanted to prove that I would be a good candidate for a solo at nationals, so I was willing to overlook Abby's inappropriate comments and choices and didn't understand why my mom was making such a big deal about it. Looking back, though, I wish that little Nia had known this solo was set up for her not to win. There was nothing competitive about the dance. I put on a great show, but I wasn't given a winning routine.

Still, Shangela, the artist of the song, became a good friend of mine shortly after that dance. She actually scared me at first. I had no idea who was strutting in with a big fur coat, hat, and blinged-out glasses. She was gorgeous and took the room by storm with her spunky personality. I hid behind Abby because I didn't know what was happening. Then all of a sudden, Shangela fell to the floor in a death drop. I had never seen that move before. After she introduced herself, I was told she was the artist behind the song "Laquifa." I thought meeting her was the coolest thing. She gave me a special part in the group dance that week after teaching me how to do a death drop, which became one of my signature moves.

I had no clue what a drag queen was before I met Shangela. I was a ten-year-old from Pittsburgh, so I was a little sheltered. Upon meeting her, I thought she was beautiful, and I wanted to be like her: fun and sassy. I didn't even know Shangela was a man dressing up as a woman until later that week, when the girls came to me and said, "Did you know Shangela is a boy?" I honestly couldn't believe it because Shangela was definitely a woman in my eyes. Our parents explained what a drag queen was, and we all thought it was pretty cool. That was my first time being exposed to the drag world, and it helped shape me into the proud ally I am today. Some of the coolest people I've met and have worked with are from the LGBTQIA+ community, and they've helped me build my confidence and come out of my shell.

I understood from my brief interaction with Shangela what it felt like to be at the top of the pyramid. I got a special part, one-on-one attention from a teacher, and choreography that showcased my talent and set me apart from others. Imagine if I'd had that experience all seven seasons! Small patterns of behavior and positive reinforcement add up. Meeting other people in the dance industry apart from *Dance Moms* and the ALDC allowed for a different perspective. I relied too heavily on Abby's measures of success in dancing. Away from her narrow-minded vision of me, I discovered an overwhelming number of people believed success was about more than having good feet.

I have met dancers and choreographers from prestigious companies and programs who made it a point to seek me out and tell me they like my dancing, they see my talent, and they want me to keep it up. These are the affirmations I hold on to when I see or hear negative and mean comments from people parroting Abby's words. I also hold on to the words written in so many books by champions who succeeded despite setbacks and obstacles in their lives. These voices kept me going. They gave me the determination to continue betting on my success. That was one of the greatest lessons I took from the show: Make your own opportunities—don't just wait for others to say it is your turn. My turn was never happening at the ALDC or on *Dance Moms*. I needed to be surrounded by people who did not use the show to define me. That was the only way I could grow, mature, and develop into my full potential.

I still recall with pride and happiness what it felt like to work with Shangela. I learned that you will find allies in the places where you least expect it. She was like my real-life fairy godmother.

I've struggled to understand why some viewers accused me of not being Black enough or not claiming my Blackness. Outside of school and dance, my life was centered around Black people and our culture. I was a part of Jack and Jill of America, a membership organization of mothers and children that focuses on nurturing future African American leaders through leadership development, civic duty, and volunteer services. Perhaps viewers assumed that I didn't embrace my Blackness because they seldom saw me interact with other Black people on the show, but I had no control over the lack of diversity in that environment. And since my family life wasn't a part of the show, my interactions with other Black people or my community weren't showcased.

I've received many comments from viewers that I was "trying to be white" or that I didn't know I was Black. As if the way that I talked or the fact that I sometimes straightened my hair meant I didn't know who I was. Trust me—I never forgot my race. If anything, that awareness was heightened by the lack of diversity at the studio and within the competition dance industry as a whole.

I always found it interesting that so many of the great dancers portrayed in media were Black, but in competition dance there were so few. That disconnect just did not make sense to me. Why did it seem like the world of competition dance dismissed the talents and merits of Black dancers? Oftentimes I would hear people make false claims about why this was: Black dancers were not technical enough, or their musicality was off, or they didn't have a dancer's body. I never thought these arguments held up. The dissonance I've noticed between the presence of talented Black dancers in the world and Black dancers in competition dance has made me wonder about the underbelly of the competition industry.

I was often one of the few Black dancers—if not the only—in many of the competitions I participated in. I felt like the token Black girl, the one held up as an example. Like "This team isn't racist! We have a Black person." Or "What do you mean there's no diversity in dance? Look at Nia!"

Being the token sucks because if you rub someone the wrong way, they're going to generalize and stereotype. There's no second chance to prove who you are. I also don't like tokenism because it means I'm the exception; I'm the Black person who is perceived as "tolerable" to white people, and I hate that. But I think people who saw me on the show thought I liked being surrounded by white people. Even worse, they assumed that because I was the token Black girl in a sea of white dancers, I didn't like being Black. That couldn't have been further from the truth. I wanted more than anything for there to be more Black dancers on my team and at competitions. I wanted other dancers I could relate to, other Black kids to dance alongside me so I didn't stick out.

I recently saw a comment online that said, "Abby only kept Nia on the show to be the token Black girl," and I chuckled. This, also, couldn't have been further from the truth. I felt like Abby had been trying to get rid of me since day one, and she certainly didn't show any compunction over the show's lack of diversity.

My tokenism extended to the dances themselves too. When there were special parts assigned in group dances, I was almost never chosen unless the decision was influenced by my race. Even then, I still had to fight for the lead. Although the "Rosa Parks" routine from season 3 was a great dance that I loved, it was very controversial for that reason. It was so well choreographed we knew it would be a winner from the start. And having the chance to represent Rosa Parks, especially after all that I had endured at the studio, meant the world to me. Given how I was typically chosen for dances of this nature, I had no doubt I would be granted the opportunity.

However, Jill (Kendall's mom) and Abby had other plans. Jill had no issue with her white daughter playing a Black civil rights activist. If the role was available, then why wouldn't Kendall be considered for it? The one time it made sense to typecast me, Abby wasn't sure who would get the part!

Rosa Parks is a historical figure renowned in Black history. Why did I have to fight Kendall for this role? Was Kendall going to perform the dance in blackface to show she was Rosa Parks? I was more than capable of performing the routine and hated any implication to the contrary. To me, the whole thing was not only ridiculous but insulting.

That whole week Abby dangled the part over my head. She would say things like, "Well, Nia, you know, you could have this part, but you're gonna have to fight for it." I am honestly surprised more people didn't catch on to her racism sooner. I ended up playing Rosa Parks in the actual dance, but the drama leading up to it was so unnecessary.

After watching the episode, I recognized a pattern of microaggressions from Jill. Interestingly enough, she never advocated for Kendall to have the roles of a slave or a maid when those characters were available, yet she fought for her daughter to get this part. (In a recent interview, Jill explains that she still sees no issue with Kendall playing Rosa Parks.[4])

This dance was one of only a handful that the producers allowed to be overtly about race. There was another dance—a beautiful contemporary piece—that was originally titled "Free at Last." In it, I was meant to play the role of a slave. We had filmed the entire episode, but then, when it was time to air, the producers worried about how the dance would be perceived. So the title of the dance was changed to "At Last," and they laid new music over the slow, hymnlike song that originally played. They even had Abby record new pickups—interview clips—discussing the piece so it didn't appear to be about race and slavery.

Though Abby was vocal about how she thought I wasn't a good dancer and the only reason our group dances won was because of Maddie, anytime we did a dance about race and I was the lead, it won. But then, Abby knew that it would. If she wanted a dance to win, she'd set it up for a win. Because of this, I sometimes felt uncomfortable doing race-related pieces. If there was a team we wanted to beat or a specific competition she wanted us to win, she would have us do a dance about race. It was as if to her, the "race card" equated to an "easy win." That never sat right with me.

There's a difference between getting chosen for a routine that celebrates your Black heritage, like the Rosa Parks dance, and being picked because you're Black and fit a negative stereotype. If a dance called for an animal, the help, a thug, a thief, a kidnapper, or a gang member, I was usually the one cast in these roles. The other girls would have solos and special parts in dances that had nothing to do with their race. They got beautiful lyrical numbers where they portrayed fairies, princesses, royalty. Eventually, I got tired of it. But when my mom voiced her opinions about this, Abby basically told us we should be grateful to even be there, as if I hadn't worked hard for my spot. My goal was to be a professional dancer and performer, so despite the unfairness of her typecasting, I put my whole heart into any routine I was given.

In addition to having controversial routines, we had some culturally inappropriate ones too. The dance that stands out to me the most was called "Tribal Council," based on Native American culture. This piece resonated with me because I have Native American ancestry on my both my mom's and my dad's side of the family (thus my middle name being Sioux). Since Abby knew this, she told me I could be the lead in this group dance. I got to wear a gold costume while everyone else wore red, and I wore a "headdress." But the dance did not reflect Native American culture. Looking back on it, the moves were a bit cliché, and I think the dance would have come off as more authentic if we had brought in a Native American instructor to teach it. The same goes for most of the Bollywood routines we performed.

Ultimately, Abby just didn't understand the cultures she was appropriating. It wasn't until season 6 that she brought in a renowned Bollywood dance teacher to choreograph a dance for us. I was grateful for the chance to learn and understand the respect for the dance and the culture from which it came.

Living under a microscope and having so many people judge me, my actions, and my identity throughout many of my formative years was brutal. I was not a character on a show—I was a young girl growing up. It was exhausting trying to do everything right. I constantly feared that I would do or say something to make me look bad, so I started to overthink everything I said or did. No decision was too small.

Despite the pressure, we still managed to come across as our authentic selves. We did not allow anyone to railroad us. My mom did a great job of protecting me and fighting for me, and I admire her for that because she always knew what to say and how to handle the hardest situations while keeping her cool. She never swore on *Dance Moms*, which is unheard of for reality TV, especially on a show like ours that had plenty of swearing. Through a plethora of emotions, she responded in an articulate, classy way, which took some serious strength. These were the skills that would benefit me later in life, when I had to control my emotions on camera, during interviews, or on social media platforms. I will be forever grateful for the way she taught me to face adversity.

One of the earliest instances of adversity and stereotyping that I experienced on the show happened in Florida during season 1.[5] We were there filming and all met up at Abby's Florida house for a pool day. Abby liked to play this game where she would get a watermelon, grease it up, and throw it into the pool. Whoever captured the watermelon and brought it out of the pool won.

We all jumped into the pool to play and were having a great time. Brooke and I brought the melon out of the water together, but Maddie was sitting in the corner crying, claiming it was because someone had kicked her. I didn't recall anyone being close to her, but since I didn't see what happened, I couldn't confirm or deny her claim.

Then, out of nowhere, her mom said I had been the one to kick her. I was shocked. I'd been nowhere near Maddie and had originally thought she was crying because she didn't win. I told everyone it wasn't me, but Melissa didn't believe me and even went as far as saying on national television that since I had brothers and was used to roughhousing, I was aggressive and had hurt Maddie. We'd all been splashing around; we were just kids having fun. But I guess that when you're a Black kid, there's a limit to how much of a good time you're allowed to have.

Melissa has apologized for things she said and did over the years. While I appreciate the apology, it doesn't excuse what she said. A small mistake for her turned into a huge strike against me.

I know that Melissa and her girls have worked on themselves to overcome past prejudices and misperceptions about people of color. Being in LA opened their eyes to matters of race because it's such a diverse city, much different from Murrysville, Pennsylvania, where they used to live. Since the rise of the Black Lives Matter movement and the murder of George Floyd in 2020, I think a lot of the girls from the show have tried to educate themselves, especially as they became adults and were able to reframe what I experienced through a more mature lens.

Whenever a Black dancer was brought on the show, I would be so happy. I was excited that I would fit in more and stand out less. But they never stayed, and I'd go back to being the only one. I didn't understand why it had to be this way. I wish the producers had scouted more Black dancers. Not doing so feels like a choice to me.

The first Black family to join *Dance Moms* after Mom and me were Nicaya and her mother, Kaya, who was known as "Black Patsy." Kaya had apparently gained her famous moniker from other moms at their current dance studio. She came to the ALDC with that name and even had it embroidered on her jacket. They appeared on the show later in season 2, and I was stoked. I had always hoped for a Black castmate, so when I saw Nicaya come into the studio, I got so excited. I looked up at my mom, who was sitting in the viewing area, and pointed to the new little Black girl, a big smile on my face. Finally, I had someone to dance with who looked like me.

The good feelings didn't last. Kaya would say negative things about my dancing like, "Nia's the weak link" or "Nicaya has way more energy than her" or "Nicaya is the real performer." It felt like she was pitting Nicaya and me against each other. This was so unnecessary. Sure, we may have been competing, but we didn't have to dislike each other. It looked bad that the only time we had another Black dancer on the team, there was drama.

Viewers were mad at my mom because they felt like she wasn't being nice to Kaya. Mom was never antagonistic toward her, but why would she be friends with someone who was constantly saying things to get her daughter replaced on the team? I do think Kaya had a change of heart after she saw how brutal the situation was and probably would have appreciated more of my mom's support.

Mom and I always thought there was space for more than one Black dancer. Couldn't Nicaya just create her own place on the team? Yet Kaya was constantly on the defense, attacking me and my mom's character. She even threatened that Nicaya would take my spot and get me kicked off the show. Someone was always trying to get that "angry Black woman" narrative out of my mom, and it felt like Kaya was willing to play into that game while Mom wouldn't. My mom had a rule that she did not want to fight with other Black women on the show because she knew that was the conflict the producers wanted. Jill, on the other hand, had no problem fighting with Kaya—and she did so constantly.

The way this played out was such a huge disappointment. I was looking for a friend, not a rival. Nicaya tried out for the ALDC elite squad, but then never returned to the team. She did appear in several other episodes, competing against our team instead of with it. There were plenty of other girls who came onto the show to be used as "rivals," but this one hit harder because I'd been the only Black dancer for so long.

The second Black girl who joined was Asia Monet Ray. Once again, I was excited to have someone on the team who looked like me. Asia was super spunky and energetic and had a whole lot of sass onstage, so we were great duet partners. We were both known for our stage presence. We worked together so well that we were able to make the most of one really bad situation we were put in.

Warming up before performing is crucial, especially for pieces involving acrobatics. Going onstage without properly preparing your body can be particularly dangerous when dances involve tricks, flips, and intricate movements that can have disastrous effects if not done correctly. At one competition, however, Asia and I were rushed onstage for our duet without being given a chance to warm up. It felt like our piece was expendable, just a filler—not all routines that we competed were televised. We could have gotten hurt, but despite the circumstances, we danced well.

After this rushed experience, a rule was implemented that ensured all of us received adequate time to warm up and rehearse before competing onstage. It is interesting to note how many rules had to be established at the expense of my mistreatment. This was a safety issue, and no one should have had to risk injury in the name of sticking to a film schedule.

I was grateful, however, for Asia's poise and partnership throughout that experience. She is a very talented dancer, and we're still friends to this day. She remained for only part of the season before leaving to film her own spin-off show, *Raising Asia.*

After Asia's departure, my mom and I recognized a pattern of production bringing in new girls or problematic parents to create drama. I believe their thinking was that viewers would get bored if they didn't bring in outsiders to spice things up, but for a dancer of color who rarely received the opportunity to dance with other girls of color, this strategy had a particularly adverse effect. It created an unnecessary rivalry instead of a comradery in a field where so few of us already exist. It was disheartening that the majority of my experiences with other Black dancers were negative or short-lived.

Mothers and Daughters

No matter how difficult things got on set, my mom was my rock through it all. She really is my best friend. When I was little, she would take me everywhere. We would go shopping together, get our hair and nails done, and go to the movies. Since I didn't have many friends in school, I would hang out with my mom most of the time. Our bond continued to grow while we were on *Dance Moms* because we endured so much together.

During the times we traveled to LA, Mom was not only my best friend but also my assistant, stylist, and chauffeur. She drove me to my acting classes, workouts, trainings, voice lessons, and anything else I was doing off set. She made sure I got to everything on time and assisted with any business that needed to be handled. People often mistook her for my manager, but she never managed me; she only helped me with meetings, appointments, and responding to emails. We talked about her role early on in my career and agreed she would not be my manager. I just wanted her to be my mom and nothing else. I saw how show business tore families apart and did not want that to happen to us. She kept my best interests at heart and never allowed money to get in the way of our relationship.

I didn't realize how amazing of a relationship I had with her until after *Dance Moms* wrapped. Though some of the girls had good relationships with their mothers, they didn't necessarily hang out together. That's the norm for a lot of teenagers; they don't want to hang out with their parents, no matter how much they love them. But my parents, specifically my mom, are my people.

Every day I look at Mom and am just in awe. Like, *Wow, you really are Wonder Woman.* It doesn't even make sense to me how she was able to do so many things and maintain the ability to treat people with kindness and respect. Though, even as I write that, I know she is also quick to remind anyone who messes with her that she's from the Bronx.

Dr. Holly Frazier is legitimately my number-one fan and biggest supporter. She always believes in me and tells me I can do whatever I put my mind to. I admit that I felt like she was a Debbie Downer when she told me she didn't think we'd get on this show because we were "too boring," but she was just trying to be realistic and prepare me for when life didn't go my way. With most things, she's absolutely in my corner. She has allowed me to take the lead in my career and make my own decisions, whether good or bad, and she has always stood by me.

This is why I get so upset whenever I hear people say she's a bad mom. I can't speak for every dancer on the show, because I know each of us had very different relationships and experiences with our mothers, but my trauma was not caused by my parents.

Now, if you want to talk about my mom letting a nine-year-old dictate what was going to happen, sure, I understand questioning that decision. But you cannot say she was a bad mom who signed me up for the show against my will or wanted her child to be a star. She never once forced me to do anything—I've always wanted this life for myself. She didn't even want to do the show in the first place; she did it for me. Nor did my parents use one penny of my money. Instead, they always made it clear the money I earned was mine and mine alone. They taught me the value of doing things for myself and working hard to get what I want. They allowed me to have the career I desired and not one that was expected of me.

Most importantly, Mom was always my champion in the face of injustice and my shoulder to cry on whenever I needed comfort and love. I've already shared countless examples of this, but some memories stand out from the rest.

One day after filming out in LA, I asked the other girls whether they had any plans and if they wanted to hang out. Despite our sometimes rocky dynamic, I desired a relationship with them because we spent so much time with one another, so I would often make bids for their companionship. They said that they didn't have any plans. I had an errand to run, so I told them to just let me know what they ended up doing, suggesting we go out for dinner.

When I didn't hear back from them, my mom and I went out and had a lovely evening. We shopped, had dinner, and walked around. It was a fun night—until I returned to the hotel and checked my phone. My heart dropped when I saw posts online that showed everyone—even Abby—hanging out with two of our favorite YouTubers. One of them was a popular female YouTuber while the other was someone we knew well and were obsessed with, Todrick Hall. We all knew and had worked with Todrick on one of his videos called "Freaks Like Me." Filming that video was when everyone heard me sing for the first time. They were shocked by how good I sounded.

The girls looked like they were having the time of their lives. I was crushed beyond words. It seemed obvious that this had been a planned event, and I'd been purposely left out. I called my dad and bawled my eyes out. I even cried myself to sleep. Mom was with me the whole time, in tears right alongside me. She felt so bad that there was nothing she could really do for her little girl, but her presence and compassion meant a lot to me.

Mom recently shared with me that she used to cry a lot while we were on the show. She told me how hard it was for her to see me get hurt over and over again. But I didn't see her cry much. She held it together in front of me most of the time. Learning that she would shed tears in private truly makes me sad. I know it had to be so hard for her. She prayed a lot, and I think that's what got her through the hard times.

The one thing she wasn't going to do was let this unjust situation slide. The next day, when we arrived at the studio, Mom went straight inside and confronted Abby and the other moms. She said, "You all blatantly lied to our faces and said you weren't hanging out, and then we go online and see all of you." She told them how much it hurt me and that I'd cried myself to sleep. It started a whole big argument, and I was shocked that everyone looked clueless and couldn't comprehend the fact that they had done something wrong. Instead, they tried to defend their actions.

I am grateful to my mother for always having my back, for taking up the task of righting wrongs she did not create. She could have sat idly by, but that wasn't her way. From taking me places to buying me things, she made sure that, no matter what, I didn't go without. With her, I always felt loved and included.

Months later, when the show aired, the female YouTuber contacted me to hang out. She hadn't realized what had happened and felt awful about it. Todrick had also been in the dark about why I wasn't there. He felt terrible as well.

People always say, "When people show you who they are, believe them." I truly believe Abby left me out on purpose. But I had the opportunity to be someone different—to be the bigger person.

So, I invited JoJo to go to the get-together with the YouTuber and me because she was the new girl and had been left out as well. The two of us, our moms, and the YouTuber all had dinner, and it was lovely. It definitely made me feel better, even though it took place months after the initial slight. This was one of the core moments that pushed JoJo and me closer as friends.

Another memorable time when Mom went above and beyond for me, I was thirteen or fourteen, and Taylor Swift was on her 1989 World Tour. Her concert was coming to Pittsburgh, and I was excited because, like the other girls, I was a huge fan. Since Maddie had been working with the pop star Sia, she had gotten tickets through her connections. She invited Kenzie and Kendall to the Taylor Swift concert with her. I was hurt by this because I would have loved to go and would have gladly paid for my own ticket, but I wasn't asked. Also, at this point there were only four of us girls who lived in and were from Pittsburgh. I was literally the one girl left out. They even brought Kendall's older sister over me.

As the night of the concert neared, they would talk about it right in front of me—constantly. Everything from what they were going to wear, to how they'd do their hair, to what time they were going to meet up . . . each conversation was salt in the wound. My mom felt bad because she saw how upset I was, so she surprised me with tickets. We went to the show and had a blast. I didn't get to go backstage and meet Taylor Swift like the others, but I did have an awesome mom who would do anything to make me feel seen and appreciated.

Though these experiences were among the most memorable, they were far from the only times my mom stepped in to make me feel better. It happened all the time on a smaller scale, like when we would do meet and greets all over the country before we started to distance ourselves from the ALDC. A meet and greet is a planned event where fans could interact with us. We'd sign autographs, take pictures, or just talk to them. Usually, they included master classes, where people got a chance to dance with us, and then we'd chat with them afterward. These events were fun, and I enjoyed getting out of the studio, traveling, and doing something fun with our supporters. However, they were also ripe with opportunities for me to be treated as "less than" the other girls.

I remember one time when Maddie, Kenzie, Kendall, and I had a meet and greet and were sitting at our table, taking pictures and signing things. A fan approached the table with her mother and handed gifts to all the girls except for me. And this wasn't just any gift—it was the most beautiful snow globe I had ever seen, featuring a little Yorkie with a pink bow in its fur. The globes were personalized, with each girl's name engraved at the bottom. My family had a Yorkie at home, so I thought it was the cutest thing ever.

I stood there waiting with a smile on my face for a gift that never came. It was extremely awkward to continue being friendly and acting happy when I was wounded. I know it sounds silly, but I was little at the time and felt heartbroken.

My mom felt so bad about the incident that she found the exact snow globe and got one made for me. It's still sitting in my room. I wonder whether the other girls still have theirs.

This was just one of many reasons why I didn't mind when Abby eventually excluded me from meet and greets. I didn't need to subject myself to further pain. Seeing people come up to us time and time again just for them to say right in front of my face that another dancer was their favorite, or all the girls selling out of their autographed photos except for me . . . these things took a toll after a while.

I have seen TikTok videos, posts, and comments addressing how I was treated in comparison to some of the other girls. Fans have even pointed out things like me being cropped out of photos that we took as a team or being left out of photos altogether. There's a *Dance Moms* promotional image that comes up for the show in which I am not pictured at all, despite my being in the seven original seasons that aired. I was surprised that people picked up on these things because for years, when I would mention to the team that I wasn't included or was cut out of the picture—literally and metaphorically—they just said I was being dramatic or sensitive. It's validating to see that others noticed too.

I had learned to like my own company and didn't expect to be popular. Other people may have joined the team to be best friends with or close to the stars, but that was never my agenda. Still, I would have liked close friends to confide in about all this.

Some people can't stand confident young Black girls, I guess because we rub them the wrong way. My mom isn't one of those people; instead, she's the reason I am such a confident person. I may not have had friends to share my struggles with, but I always had her. I also had fans; despite the people who were unkind, many were lovely and did give me notes and presents. I appreciated all of them. I kept each piece of fan mail and art people sent me during my time on the show.

I feel bad that my mother had to endure so much to support my dreams. She didn't ask to be on the show and actually tried to talk me out of it before we auditioned. I'm grateful to know that, despite her feelings, she came along for the ride anyway and has no regrets. But I know it had to break her heart seeing me go through all of this. It was more than any child should have to endure. To hear people criticize and be mean to your kid isn't easy, especially when it's coming from so many people, both on set and online. No one wants to see their child struggle with that.

I know she's happy with where we are now, but boy, was the journey rough at times—not just because it was difficult to watch me but because she also endured challenges personally. She isn't someone who needs to have best friends everywhere she goes, but we were spending so much time on the road and in rehearsals that having some kind of comradery would have made things more bearable for her as well. The cast were all experiencing similar things, so that should have brought us together, bonded us, instead of tearing us apart. But the set became like a weird game of teacher's pet. People would say or do anything to get Abby's favor—especially the moms.

Recently I saw a clip from the show of Jill talking to Melissa. Melissa was frazzled because the moms were getting under her skin, and she said to Jill, "Nia has privates. Does anyone ever say [anything about] that?" to which Jill responded, "Obviously Nia is no threat to anybody."[1] Though Mom wasn't there for this conversation, she had to hear these sorts of awful comments all the time. Sometimes about me, and sometimes about her.

In footage from that same episode, when my mom, along with some of the other moms, tried to confront Jill about the underhanded ways she sought to buy Abby's favor, Jill lashed out and said, "Holly, this bothers you because you've been an absentee mom—let's face it."[2] This was such a loaded comment because it builds on the rhetoric that Black mothers are unfit and that because a Black mom works, it means she isn't in her children's lives. But my mom had given up her career for me—the very opposite of an absentee mom.

I'm a firm believer that you don't have to put someone down to build someone else up. Mom taught me that. Everyone has their own way of processing and handling transgressions and slights. Mom and I have tried to take each and every hurt on the chin and just keep being ourselves.

Because of everything happening on-screen, though, we started having issues at home. Being on television definitely put a strain on my family, especially my older brother, EJ. I hadn't realized the impact of my mom and me being on the show. The middle school and high school years are important for a child and their development; it's a time of transition during which they need love, guidance, and support more than ever. Due to our commitment to *Dance Moms*, my mom missed some monumental moments in EJ's life, like prom, school dances, football and lacrosse games—important milestones of his youth. I feel bad for taking her away from him, not just because she missed out on so much but because it ruptured my relationship with him for a good chunk of my time on the show. He couldn't understand why my work was so important. Why I was getting all the attention, leaving nothing for him.

When I finally got to hang out with our family during downtimes, EJ would get really mad at me, and we argued constantly. At family functions, if he was talking to my mom and I tried to join in the conversation, he would get upset. "You have Mom all the time," he'd say. "So back off during my time." His response hurt my feelings, and I found myself lashing out at him because I didn't understand where he was coming from. I was too young to have empathy for his experience; I thought he was just being mean.

While Mom was busy protecting me and being by my side every day, she couldn't do the same for him. As time went on, the long travel periods meant my relationship with my brother suffered even more. This was especially true in season 6, when my mom and I would stay in LA for four to five months at a time. EJ also didn't like how everyone at school knew his mom was on TV. I can't imagine how hard it must've been for him to grow up like that. The world got to see my mom every week, but EJ saw her only a few months out of the year.

During this season, my family had come out to visit my mom and me in LA. While they were there, I was invited to go to the iHeartRadio Music Awards, along with a plus-one. I thought this might be the perfect opportunity to spend some alone time with EJ, giving us a chance to reconnect. So I asked him to come with me. I missed him and wanted to be close again, so I was thrilled when he agreed. He sounded excited and couldn't wait to go. I looked forward to finally doing something fun with him.

This was the first awards show I'd ever been invited to without the rest of the cast. Stepping out of the car and onto the red carpet was like something out of a dream. I walked the carpet, and EJ got to see what happens at these types of events. We met a host of celebrities, people we'd always admired, like the Chainsmokers, Marshmello, Fifth Harmony, Shawn Mendes, Miley Cyrus, and Meghan Trainor. Everyone was there. EJ got a glimpse of my world, and he was really proud of how far I'd come. It was a once-in-a-lifetime experience that we got to share together.

I won't say our relationship magically healed overnight, but this was a step in the right direction. Seeing me in this light changed EJ's perspective and helped him understand the pressures I dealt with and the duties I had to fulfill for the show. It also showed him that all this hard work and sacrifice was paying off. I was elated to know that after everything I had put him through, he was genuinely happy for me.

Now that we're older, our relationship has gotten much better. EJ is now one of my best friends. We hang out together when I'm home and go to lunch, the movies, and games. He'll come visit me in LA sometimes too. I even went with him to approve the ring he picked out for his girlfriend. When I shared that I was writing a book, he was so supportive. He thought it was a great idea and was proud I was taking on this venture. Like the rest of my family, he agreed it was time to share my story.

I still feel bad about my mother's absence from our family, and my part in that is something that will forever haunt me. I can't shake the feeling that it was selfish of me to take her away, and though EJ and I are close now, it still weighs heavily on me. I sometimes wonder if I would choose to go down this road again, and honestly, I'm not sure that I would. I don't think I could handle putting my family through that again.

I've said it before, but it truly took a village to raise us kids. My grandparents, nannies, and family friends all helped to make sure our family stayed together. My dad did his best to hold down the fort when my mom and I were away, but he was working a full-time job with late nights. Just like me, my brothers had to grow up fast and figure things out on their own. The public has little idea of how being on TV and working on a reality show affects not just your life but the lives of everyone around you.

It's natural to look back on situations and wonder whether you could have done things differently. I'm sure my parents have those feelings about themselves, but for me, they did everything possible to support not only my dreams and successes but my brothers' as well. Yes, I dealt with some pretty difficult challenges in my journey to becoming an entertainer, but those experiences only made me stronger. Those trying times made the bond between my mom and me unbreakable.

I will never forget that Taylor Swift concert or the many times I felt excluded, nor will I forget the subsequent dinners and awesome hangouts my mom and I planned to fill that void. Though the memories are painful, I am glad I can replace some of them with positive experiences. My mom and I were, and always will be, two peas in a pod. If the girls or their moms didn't want to hang out with us, she made it okay. She taught me not to allow other people's actions to cause me to feel insecure about myself. I'm really happy she did that because it helped me to channel those hurt feelings into motivation. Eventually I learned not to let the girls, their moms, or Abby get the best of me.

My mom is the epitome of a great mother. I could probably fill these pages just with the lessons she bestowed upon me. However, I'll sum her up by saying she is a protector, a nourisher, and an inspiration. It's still difficult for me to watch the show, but of the few episodes I've seen over the years, my biggest takeaway is gratitude for my mother's love. I saw how some of the moms treated their daughters and, in turn, how their daughters treated others. We were kids, so it was up to our parents to teach us better. I'm not saying anyone was intentional with their cruelty, but it's hard for me to comprehend how mothers allowed their daughters to behave that way and to treat others so poorly for no reason—at least none known to me. I am thankful to my mom for teaching me to be a good person and to treat others with kindness and respect.

Even now, so many years later, she is my confidant, my best friend, and the person I love spending time with. She is a rock star, and I love her more and more each day.

For this, I will always be blessed.

12

Old Patterns, New Opportunities

Being a dancer is not for the faint of heart, even in the best of situations. Given how bad things were at the ALDC during season 5, I did not trust Abby with my training anymore. I was sick and tired of people seeing me as the weak link. It also seemed to me that Abby had begun to mentally check out. Most of our routines had become mundane; we would do the same jumps, turns, and leaps in all of our pieces, and our technique was really suffering. We weren't even properly warming up anymore, leaving our bodies hurting and significantly increasing our risk of injury. It was a mess.

Because I knew my technique was plateauing, I decided to train on my days off. I trained hard so no one could continue to say I was a bad dancer. I scheduled privates outside of what I did on the show and at the studio. I also took Pilates classes, ballet classes, and technique classes, and I would do strength training and flexibility exercises every night before I went to sleep, focusing mostly on my legs and feet. I had a village of people helping me to become a better dancer. My personal trainer, Tadeo Arnold, helped me work out and stay in shape, and I had standing private lessons with Richard Elszy, who helped me work on flexibility, strength, and stamina, as well as turns and jumps. I also was nurtured by Kristin McQuaid, who helped me with my dance concept videos on YouTube by choreographing, directing, and even funding them.

Around this time, I met Chloe and Maud Arnold, sisters who founded a tap group called the Syncopated Ladies. They graduated from Columbia and are recognized all over the world for their tap dancing. They run a boot camp and provide scholarships for kids to study dance. They're terrific people, and so talented. They inspire me because tap is such a male-dominated field, and they have paved their own lane in the business.

Chloe and Maud asked me to be a part of their dance video for the song "Formation." It was a tap routine, and dancers from all over the world learned and recorded themselves performing the same steps. The clips were then compiled into one video. I was honored to be included in a trio with the sisters. They even put me in the center despite them being tap stars. The video garnered millions of views and was featured on Beyoncé's Facebook page. I was finally coming into my own, and the feeling was incredible.

I was focused on building my own network in LA, and meeting Chloe and Maud was only the beginning. My outside trainers, instructors, and mentors helped to ground me during a time when I felt so disconnected. I had even befriended Ava Michelle, who was brought onto the show as a rival. We had taken some of the same acting classes and realized how much we had in common. After that, we would hang out whenever time allowed.

People finally saw my talent for themselves and realized that I wasn't a bad dancer; I just wasn't always given the same opportunities as others. I remember in season 1, a record label came to the studio looking for dancers for a music video by an artist named Lux, who is a tall, blond white woman. The girl they wanted to cast would play Lux as a child. Clearly, I wasn't going to be considered for the role since I looked nothing like her, but no one would outright say that. I had to try out like everyone else. The role was given to Chloé, who was perfect for it. Still, I wondered when my turn to do the cool, fun things would come.

The fuss surrounding the Joffrey Ballet School scholarship left me feeling similarly frustrated. Founded in the 1950s, the Joffrey Ballet School in New York City is one of the most prestigious dance schools in the world. We were given the opportunity in season 2 to audition for a scholarship. Thinking about it now, it was odd that we were even given the chance to audition, since most of us didn't have high-level ballet training. At ALDC we took ballet classes once or twice a week, but these prestigious intensives are usually reserved for dancers who primarily do ballet.

The only person on the team who had extensive ballet training was Chloé, so the opportunity was most in line with her talent and skills. At the time, I felt like I was set up to fail. I was in no way qualified for the scholarship, and Abby knew it. She told each of us what to do in the audition—and let me tell you, if Abby told you to do something, you had to do it. The other girls were doing turns and beautiful jumps, showing off their flexibility. I, meanwhile, was told to do a death drop and jazz moves, which I knew were not what a ballet school would be looking for. After the show aired, fans grilled me online, saying things like, "Why would Nia death drop for the Joffrey Ballet School audition?" I read those comments and felt so disheartened, given I'd had no choice in the matter. Anything less than what I was asked to do would have gotten me in big trouble. I can laugh about it now, but that moment still haunts me because of how embarrassed I was.

Then there was a dance magazine that came to the studio to do a schoolgirl-themed photoshoot with us. Maddie played the teacher's pet, and Kendall was chosen to play the mean girl. We were told they'd choose one of us to be on the cover of the magazine. When I was assigned the role of a gymnast, I knew it wasn't going to be the cover girl. A gymnast is not necessarily what you would think of when you picture a schoolgirl theme.

Later on, in season 5, a photographer came to the set to take professional headshots of us. Every other girl was given ample time to get that perfect shot. But, as the girl assigned to go last, I wasn't given as much time as the other girls to get my photos done. The photographer had to wrap things up.

Abby decided it wasn't worth staying for my portraits and, on her way out the door, told the photographer, "Oh, you don't have to spend much time on her because she's not gonna be bookable." Now I not only had little time left but also no coach to help pose me, in addition to her hurtful words swimming through my head.

"Ignore her," my mom told me. "She's just being her typical self." Of course, Abby would later deny any wrongdoing and say that *we* were trying to sabotage *her.*

Despite her attempts to break my spirit, my headshots came out beautifully.

Years later, the script had flipped. During season 6, I was given a fantastic opportunity to do a spread for *Seventeen* magazine. They'd reached out to the show wanting recommendations for a few girls to be featured in their February 2016 issue. Abby gave them her suggestions, which didn't include me. She even tried to talk them out of choosing me, but the magazine handpicked me to join Maddie and Kendall.

The photoshoot was so much fun, and I felt absolutely beautiful. It was one of the rare moments on *Dance Moms* when I was genuinely happy. I got to feel special, and to be chosen meant the world to me. Truly it was the boost of confidence I needed. Everyone on set was kind and excited to meet me, and everything from my outfits to my makeup and hairstyles to the direction of the shoot was perfect. It reminded me of the feeling I had when shooting the video for my debut single.

While we were in LA, I started making dance videos for my YouTube channel. I originally began the channel to showcase my music, but now I shared videos of everything from stretching to dancing to makeup and hair tutorials or just day-to-day stuff like hanging out with my family or going on vacation. I even posted behind-the-scenes footage from the show. Having that control brought me great joy. It was like I was producing my own shows, and I got to decide what I was doing.

When I started to post my dance videos, I saw a shift in how fans of the show saw me. They watched my videos repeatedly and were shocked to see me dancing in this light. I was finally getting comments telling me what an amazing dancer I was. Viewers were confused as to why I wasn't doing good choreography like this on the show. Through these videos, I found more of the validation I was seeking.

With such a positive response, I began investing more time, energy, and money into making content for my channel. I wanted people to see me dancing and dancing well. Making videos became a passion of mine, and my little brother, Will, helped me by editing my content. I loved that we'd found something we could work on together.

From there, I joined a new platform called Musical.ly, which later became TikTok. I would dance, do silly skits, or feature some of the girls from the show, and people loved it. I think fans liked seeing me doing things outside of *Dance Moms*. They got a better glimpse of my personality, and I was able to showcase my talents.

I have heard people have written dissertations about *Dance Moms*, and I can believe it. There is a lot to unpack there. In many ways it is a microcosm of American society. Watching it, you can draw a lot of parallels about equity, privilege, stereotypes, bullying, and power. I understood the value of media literacy, which is why I took matters into my own hands and controlled what I could on my YouTube channel. People needed to see a different representation of me rather than take what *Dance Moms* portrayed at face value. Social media became a great outlet, where I could build community and just be myself. My posts started opening doors for me, and I managed to book some amazing gigs.

Even as I got better and clearly held my own in group dances, some people held Abby's words in such high regard that they could not fix their eyes to see me for what I was capable of. I knew I didn't have great solos that showed off my abilities, but I did the group dances every single week and kept up just fine. Still, some fans would just repeat what they heard Abby say. When I'd see comments under clips of Maddie dancing that said things like "My eyes are trained to watch Maddie," all I could think was, *Yes, they literally* were *trained to watch her.* Abby had trained viewers to think highly of Maddie and look only at her.

Abby had so much influence over the way viewers perceived us. If Maddie made a mistake, the sentiment was "Everyone makes mistakes" or "Maddie never makes mistakes, so it's okay." I, on the other hand, wasn't given the same grace because viewers were trained to focus on my alleged shortcomings.

This is why I always joke with my family that if I ever get the chance to do a TED Talk, my topic will be media literacy, and I'll use *Dance Moms* as an example. What you watch and listen to can influence the way you see things.

And this doesn't only apply to the things you see and hear through a screen. In season 6, episode 12, Abby chose Maddie and Brynn to each have their own trio, and they got to pick their partners. There were seven girls, so with this setup, one person was obviously going to be left out. At the end of the selection, JoJo and I were the last girls standing, and Maddie had the final pick. She chose JoJo over me, driving home the point that even the girls thought I was the weakest link. I wish they would've fought against Abby's messaging and hyped me up, but no one had my back. It seemed like everyone was brainwashed.

So you can understand how my dance videos on YouTube and TikTok became such a significant force for good in my life. I was finally getting the opportunity to change the narrative.

Another mentor I'm indebted to is Debbie Allen, an award-winning producer, director, writer, actor, dancer, and choreographer who has a star on the Hollywood Walk of Fame. She has directed and choreographed for legends like Michael Jackson, Mariah Carey, James Earl Jones, Whitney Houston, Lena Horne, and more.[1]

Working with Ms. Allen was a dream. I first met her when I auditioned for her summer program in LA during the first season of *Dance Moms*. I believe I was about ten at the time. She had an amazing summer intensive workshop where dancers would take all types of dance classes. There, I formed a bit of a relationship with Ms. Allen; even though she didn't teach all the classes, she was very much involved in the day-to-day activities at the school. It was an experience I'll never forget.

During season 6 of *Dance Moms*, Abby decided that she didn't want to be a part of *Dance Moms* anymore and told producers she was going to resign. This was by far one of the craziest things she had done, and we all speculated that her decision had more to do with her pending legal issues than her unhappiness on the show. We filmed episode 5 at Debbie Allen Dance Academy that week. I was excited to return to Ms. Allen's studio since I already had a connection with her. I am a huge fan of hers and the work she has done for Black dancers. I also loved her studio and her teaching style—strict, but not malicious—and the way she gave feedback with good intentions. It was kind of surreal working with her, too, because she's a living legend.

Kalani and I did a duet to an African dance routine called "Isolations," choreographed by Aisha Frances with assistance from Anindo Marshall. I was super nervous; we didn't have much time to learn the choreography, and this was a style of dance I had not performed before. I had taken African dance classes but never actually done an African dance piece.

Abby showed up to watch us perform. Afterward, Kalani and I went to the dressing room, and Abby said that Kalani looked more African than me onstage. I remember thinking, *What does that even mean?* Unlike previous times when I was able to brush off her racially charged comments, I was highly offended by this statement. How dare she say I wasn't good at being my own race! Ridiculous.

Season 6 was also when Maddie and Kenzie left the show. I was shocked at first since Maddie was Abby's favorite, but after I had a moment to process the news, I realized the writing had been on the wall. Maddie was always off doing her own thing, so she wasn't on the show as much anymore. She had outgrown *Dance Moms.* Regardless, their departure hit me hard. The three of us had been the only OG cast members left. Now that they were gone, I was the last one standing.

As the season wrapped, I felt completely and utterly burned out. My routine had become monotonous, and enduring a continuous toxic situation left me on edge. I never knew what was going to happen next, and I didn't think I could take it anymore. The anxiety. The fear. I just wanted to be a regular teenager and enjoy doing regular teenage things. Dancing felt like a job I no longer wanted. Performances that previously thrilled me had become a giant ball of stress. In the past, I couldn't wait to find out where we'd be traveling to each week. Now I marked the calendar in anticipation of my next break so I could go home and spend time with my family. I was so tired. I wanted to be done with it all.

But then, at the end of the season, something I never thought possible happened.

We were on set at Abby's studio in LA, and I was told to go into the den area. When I arrived, I saw a cake that said "Congratulations, Nia" and an open laptop. I was so confused. What was happening? Although we'd wrapped for the night, the cameras were still rolling.

My manager pressed play on a video on the laptop. On the screen was the cast of an off-Broadway show called *Trip of Love*, and they shouted, "Welcome, Nia! We can't wait to take this trip with you."

My heart was racing. *This can't be for real!* I thought. *I haven't even auditioned for the show.* It was a direct book, meaning the director, James Walski, handpicked me for the role.

My manager explained, "You're going to spend your summer living in New York City to perform in an off-Broadway show."

It was such a huge surprise. As she told me the details, I couldn't contain my excitement. This was something I had worked for my entire life. I started crying on the spot, which made others tear up too. Even Abby gave me a hug, which was rare, especially at this point in our relationship. It was a special moment. I have a video of the whole announcement, but I don't think I've ever posted it. Maybe one day I'll share it.

Trip of Love is a 1960s coming-of-age story about a young girl who journeys down the rabbit hole of love in a time of war. I was brought on as a featured dancer, but I got to both dance and sing. The *Trip of Love* team found my mom and me an apartment in Hell's Kitchen in Manhattan, on Forty-Third Street. The theater was located on Forty-Second Street, so I could walk to work every day. I worked closely with the director and choreographer, who taught me the entire production in two weeks. It was intense but such a breath of fresh air.

We had a one-week break before the show began, and my family used that time to take a quick vacation on a Disney cruise. Mom had planned this trip twice but had to cancel both times because of the *Dance Moms* schedule. We finally had a week to make it happen, and it was absolutely magical. Returning to New York, I felt refreshed and ready to make my off-Broadway debut.

My first performance was just for the media before my official debut show. They came and took all sorts of pictures and videos to promote the show. I saw for myself how much my presence encouraged more patrons to attend. When I was first notified about the role, I came to the theater to see the show, and less than half the seats were filled. The announcement about my involvement with the show garnered a lot of buzz, and the director felt confident we could fill the seats. And we did! My debut show was sold out.

I had an incredible run, and it was cool to see that people actually came to the theater for me, especially since the cast was chock-full of working actors. I even got to work with Darlene Love, a major Broadway star who made a guest appearance in our last few shows.

The whole experience was unbelievable. The show was dance heavy, and I got to sing in an ensemble, perform solo dance parts, and be part of a duet. Though I was the youngest person onstage, everyone was nice, gracious, and easy to work with. I didn't take one moment for granted.

I think the other cast members had a positive experience working with me too. I remember one castmate told me, "We were kind of worried when we heard that you were coming because you're on a reality TV show. We didn't know what to expect."

Another said, "It has been so cool and fun to see how much you enjoy this, which reminds us how much we love doing this too."

Someone else told me that my love for the arts was like a breath of fresh air. I'm sure this was because I kept telling them that this job was the best thing ever. I always came in with a smile on my face and couldn't wait to see what the day's performance held. This was my first theater job, and I was enamored with the experience.

Not only was the cast amazing, but my costumes were gorgeous. Oh my gosh. I was used to raggedy ensembles that often fell apart, but here we had costumes that were made by a

Tony Award–winning designer. I also had clothes and shoes that were custom-made to fit me. I was taught how to properly pin-curl my hair for underneath my wig cap and how to secure a wig with very few bobby pins. There was someone tasked with helping me put on my mic, and a team of people assisted with our quick changes offstage.

Quick changes in general weren't new to me. I was used to a one-number quick change during recitals, but this was a whole new ball game. There was one number where we had only fifteen seconds to change costumes. I would dance offstage and change in the wings. Sometimes my hair would change, too, which meant switching wigs. There was even a dance where we quick-changed behind a moving prop onstage! Everything was planned to a T to make sure things went seamlessly.

So much thought and effort goes into a live show, and pulling everything off with precision is part of what makes it so exciting. Sometimes things don't go according to plan—you don't hit your mark, you don't make your quick change, you get hurt. But the show always goes on, no matter what. You make it look easy so the audience can't tell your dress is maybe not zipped up all the way or that you forgot a line. I love how chaotic it is. You never know what's going to happen.

Every night was such a thrill because there was a different audience with each show, which came with new energy; no two shows were ever exactly the same. I craved that energy. It's what I live for and have been hungry for ever since I left that production. It was a blessing to be a part of something like that.

Lots of friends and family came to see me in *Trip of Love*. Even Abby came to see the show before it closed. Despite us not being on the best of terms, it was nice to have her there. A part of me still yearned for her approval, and it felt good to hear her say she was proud of me.

Kalani came, as did Ava Michelle, and Kaeli Ware, who was on a few episodes. Jojo had tried to come, but the show closed before she was able to make it. It meant a lot to me to have some of my castmates see me living out my dream.

The show ran for about six weeks, and it was the best summer of my life. I had such a blast in *Trip of Love* that returning for the final season of *Dance Moms* was the furthest thing from my mind. I was loving not having that gut-wrenching feeling going into work. I felt appreciated and seen. The experience opened my eyes to the life—and career—waiting for me outside of *Dance Moms*.

To anyone who had ever doubted me for my dance abilities on and off the show, my off-Broadway success was proof that I had undeniable talent. I was now a professional dancer and had earned an actor's equity card, which is a membership card from the Actors' Equity Association you receive as part of an actors' union in theater. No one else on the show had accomplished that.

Ultimately, my dream had come true because I believed in myself. I believed I could do hard things. For so long I had felt overwhelmed by the perception that the world was against me. But once I came to terms with what I wanted, and I believed I was deserving of it, I was able to own my success.

I was no longer striving to fit in. I didn't need to prove to anyone that I was a good dancer. I was dancing for myself. I was finding joy in performing again.

And in the wake of that joy, I made a decision: I didn't want to return to *Dance Moms*. I'd gotten a glimpse of what my life could look like without the show, and it was beautiful. Despite all I'd been through during my tenure on *Dance Moms*, this was the first time I actually wanted to leave.

I'd always found the bright side to things, found a reason to stay. It's why I was the last original girl from the show left. For six years I'd pushed through, honored my contracts, and stuck it out, putting in 100 percent dedication even though I was not being appreciated nor making enough money for what I endured. It seemed like Abby barely came to work, and yet she was making significantly more than any of us girls. She would even gloat sometimes that she was being paid $20,000 an episode. Meanwhile, we were working overtime and not making half of that. I wouldn't even be able to pay for college tuition with what I'd made from *Dance Moms*.

I was just done with it all. More than ever before, I was confident that a bright future awaited me outside of the ALDC.

Saying Goodbye

I kept telling my mom that I didn't think I could go back, not after such an unimaginable summer. I got to sing, I got to dance, I got to learn and feel good about myself. What could be better? I was also working on my first movie in Texas. That entire experience furthered the point that knowing the right people could put me in a position to receive the opportunities I deserved. It wasn't Abby who got me the role; it was my tenacity and hard work. The brand endorsements, movies, performances, red carpet events, and everything else I'd accomplished thus far were all my accomplishments. The fact that my off-Broadway role had been tailored for me was the cherry on top. I had faith that there would be more opportunities like this coming my way.

I no longer needed *Dance Moms*. I felt liberated.

So, when the network reached out to confirm season 7 would be happening, I couldn't have cared less. In my mind, I wasn't returning. I'd already mapped out what I was going to say, and we had our lawyer on standby just in case.

When producers approached us with our contract agreement for the season, I told them I wasn't interested. But then I started having second thoughts. I had only one season left in my contract. Did I really want to break it? I had made it this far. Was I really going to quit after all of that, or would I finish what I'd started?

I talked it over with my parents, and we decided I would return only if they increased my pay. Since we didn't get residuals and the network made millions off the show and reruns, I knew they could afford to pay me more. It didn't take long for them to agree to an increase, but I wasn't the only one who would get a raise. The network decided to increase all the main girls' pay.

I can't pretend that I wasn't upset. I was the only OG left. My seniority and dedication to the show throughout the years should have resulted in a certain level of respect. But I couldn't harp on that. I wanted to get through this last season so I could move on and close that chapter of my life.

When I walked back onto set that seventh season, I definitely had more confidence. A lot had changed in my life. I was homeschooled for seventh and eighth grade, but I was now starting high school, and for my freshman year, I attended an all-girls Catholic school called Oakland Catholic in Pittsburgh. It was actually the sister school to the one my brothers attended, Central Catholic. My freshman year, my older brother, EJ, was a senior, and my sophomore year, Will was a freshman. I loved that a lot of the girls knew my older brother because I was seen more as "Evan's little sister" than as "Nia from *Dance Moms*." I was doing so well in school that I was in honors math and science classes. I'd been there for a year and a half, and I don't know how I even made it that far since I missed a lot of school to film in LA and had to do most of my work remotely, but I was thriving.

Then, during the second part of season 7, Laurieann Gibson came onto the show to teach us after Abby left. She is a tough cookie but also someone who genuinely wanted to help me get better. Laurieann is a choreographer, director, TV personality, singer, actress, and dancer. She has choreographed for musical greats like

Michael Jackson, Alicia Keys, Lady Gaga, and Beyoncé. She was also featured on shows like *Making the Band* and *So You Think You Can Dance*. Laurieann saw my potential and gave me the final boost of confidence I'd been missing.

The first week she was there, Laurieann lined all of us up, pointed to me, and said about Abby, "What do you feel that she's held you back from?" I explained that I'd been at the ALDC and on the show the longest and that she was so hard on me that it seemed as if she hated me and was trying to crush me. Laurieann asked me how I felt about that. I began to speak, a smile plastered on my face, but as the words came out of my mouth, my mom interrupted me and said, "It's okay to show your emotions."

My smile cracked, and I got choked up. I started to cry and couldn't hold back the tears. In my mind, I was thinking, *Suck it up, suck it up. Don't cry, don't cry. Never let them see you cry!* Yet I couldn't stop, nor could I move. My feet were planted to the floor, preventing me from seeking solace in the bathroom as I normally did, away from the girls and the scope of cameras. As I cried, Laurieann walked over to me and said, "No one has endured what I've endured, but it made me faster, bigger, stronger, better. They told me that I couldn't, and I did . . . and not only do I get in, I dominate. I'm not afraid of Abby Lee, she should be afraid of me."[1]

After that moment, I couldn't stop crying the whole week. I don't think I realized how bad I was hurting inside. Maybe that was the beginning of my healing.

During Laurieann's second week with us, she choreographed a duet that I had been chosen for, but at the last minute she decided to replace me with another dancer. I'd been elated when we got a new member of the dance team, Camryn Bridges, who came onto the show for my final season. Camryn and I became fast friends, and I was happy to finally have a comrade on the team who also happened to be Black. Typically, I would have been hurt by the switch, but I wasn't upset at all by it. Laurieann didn't put me down or tell me I was horrible; she simply stated that Camryn would be a better fit, and I was fine with that. I think Camryn may have had more energy, which is what Laurieann was looking for.

Laurieann was determined to spark the fire back in me after what I had endured with Abby. Camryn was still new on the team and had a light that Abby hadn't managed to snuff out before she left. I have great respect for teachers, and though Laurieann wasn't warm or fuzzy, she was respectful to us. She didn't call me a bad dancer, didn't say I had bad feet, didn't say anything to put me down. She knew how to give constructive criticism without breaking my spirit. I thoroughly enjoyed working with her. It was amazing to work with a Black woman whose industry skills are world-renowned. Her teaching style and choreography were different from what I was used to, and for once I was able to see myself reflected in her. I opened up and relaxed, no longer afraid to say or do the wrong thing. I remembered what it was like to be free and let myself enjoy the moment.

Working with her those three weeks opened the floodgates of my emotions. I found myself crying off and on throughout her time with us. The other girls were surprised by my sudden bouts of emotion because they'd hardly ever seen me cry. But those feelings had been repressed for almost seven years, and now they couldn't help breaking through the cracks of the facade I had been hiding behind. The stress, the pain, the anger, the loneliness, the disappointment, the insecurities—I was letting it all out.

I wasn't worried anymore that I'd get in trouble if I showed emotion. Instead, I was shown that the opposite could be true. That emotion brought passion and motivation, and I was encouraged to leave my emotions on the dance floor, to let them out so I could release them and heal from past traumas. I was letting go of the ALDC, both figuratively and emotionally.

While I didn't necessarily want to break down in front of everyone, I'm glad I did because they got to see a different side of me. Even the producers worried about my well-being. Everyone was so used to me being strong and put together. This was a softer, less solid me. But that's the thing: So many of us are like this. We suppress our emotions when we're overworked, don't get enough sleep, or are frustrated. We don't want to upset anyone, so we put ourselves through the wringer, trying to prove a point. Meanwhile, we are killing ourselves from the inside out. We don't allow ourselves rest and vulnerability, which can be exhausting.

I remember at practice, Laurieann said something like, "You guys are dancing like robots. You need to break free. . . . You are so mechanical, trying to be perfect. You're not actually dancing." That is what we were used to. As long as it made Abby happy, we went through the motions, did whatever we needed to do to make it through to the end. Having the chance to work with other choreographers was the step I needed to disembark not just from the show but from the toxic ALDC mindset.

What saddened me most that last season was the treatment Camryn received from Abby when she was around. Since Camryn had a darker complexion, Abby would constantly talk about her skin tone. One time, she told Camryn she was so dark that she should paint the bottom of her feet because they were lighter and stood out. Who says something like that?

Camryn is a beautiful and talented girl, and I truly loved dancing with her. She made me a better dancer. I really had to bring it when dancing with her because she was sharp and her technique was great. She made me want to work harder. It was refreshing to see someone enter the team with so much passion. She didn't deserve the awful behavior from Abby. Nor did she deserve the typecasting that went on in the dances she was chosen for.

At one competition, we performed a piece based on the movie *The Help*. Of course, Camryn and I played the workers while the other girls were rich socialites. At the end of the dance, I rebelled and left my position as the help, while Camryn's character stayed. Although we won, I still ended up at the bottom of the pyramid. Abby said it was because she didn't like my rebellious character's nature—as if she hadn't assigned that role to me!—while she praised Camryn's subservient role. She was always fond of making sure people knew their place.

That wasn't the only dance that Abby put a damper on. We worked with Aisha Francis, an extremely talented and very accomplished choreographer, on an incredible piece called "The Last Dance." A former LA Lakers cheerleader, she's gone on to choreograph for artists like Rihanna, Janet Jackson, Normani, and Beyoncé. She has also danced alongside Prince, Chris Brown, Ciara, Kid Rock, Cher, and Jay-Z, and the list goes on. She specializes in choreography wearing high heels, so she teaches her students not only how to do to the moves but how to perfect them in four-inch stilettos.

At the time, most of us were like fifteen or sixteen years old—much older than we'd been when we performed the "Topless

Showgirls" routine—yet Abby berated the dance, criticizing the tone and look for the show. I found this comical given how many inappropriate routines she'd had us do over the years. We completely tuned her out because the choreography made us feel confident. Abby's biggest issue was probably regarding our costumes: We wore fishnet stockings with the heels and a tiny bra and shorts. But this type of look was nothing new; we'd been wearing outfits like this since we were ten years old.

The movements, based on *Chicago*-style musical theater and jazz steps, were fresh and fun, not boring and stale like so many of our previous dances. I remember all of us being upset because the moms of the minis (the new dancers Abby had brought onto the show because she said we were too old and washed up), along with Ashlee and her daughter, Brynn, bad-mouthed us about our costumes and choreography, insinuating we were like prostitutes who sold our bodies for fame. We did our best not to focus on the negativity and just have fun with the routine, but it was hard.

By the end of season 7, my Musical.ly platform had gained a significant following, and I was starting to work with big brands. I had a campaign with Target and was contracted to work with them for almost a year to help launch a new line of children's clothing. As part of their Art Class collection, several other influencers and I got to travel to the Target headquarters in Minneapolis, where we worked with designers to create our own outfits.

My mom and I had been there for only one day when she received a call from the other dance moms, letting us know they were walking out of the studio. They told us they were no longer dancing for the ALDC. Abby had completely shifted her attention to the minis. She was treating everyone horribly, and that was when she showed up to the studio at all. The moms asked my mom, "Are you with us?"

My mom told them, "Absolutely."

We never set foot in an ALDC dance studio again.

We did, however, continue to be filmed as dancers for the show through the end of the season. My last solo performance with the show would be a routine entitled "I Need No One." It was another of my favorites. This dance was choreographed by Cheryl Burke and her assistant, Ryan Ramirez. Cheryl began dancing at the age of four and was the first female pro to win *Dancing with the Stars*. She was fantastic to work with, and her teaching style was quite refreshing. You could tell that she really respected us. I think she saw some of herself in us because she'd come from a place where she'd been criticized as well.

We were finally filming the last episode of the show, and I was a bag of mixed emotions. On the one hand, I was relieved, but I was also sad to be leaving behind something I had been a part of for so many years. Even though it was an emotional day, I was ready to go. The whole day the producers kept saying, "Well, you never know, this might not be the last episode" or "This might not be your last season," but it very much was my last. Even if the network decided to do another season, my seven-year commitment was up, and I was mentally and emotionally tired. This had been a long time coming. I was ready to close this chapter of my life.

The producers insisted that we were going to miss doing the show. I was adamant that I wouldn't. Even now, I do not miss it one bit. Still, that whole day felt weird. As I performed my last solo and last group piece, I was very aware that this would be the last time dancing with these girls—my last competition ever. In a bittersweet victory, both my solo and the group dance won first place.

And then it was over.

I'd survived and conquered and redeemed myself in the end. I had closure. I never had to work with Abby again. And yet, when we wrapped, I went to the dressing room and cried my eyes out. When it was time to leave, we all hugged, then turned off the makeup lights and went home.

With season 7 behind me, I no longer had a dance home, which meant there was nowhere for me to practice, train, or rehearse. I genuinely did not know what to do with myself. Yes, I was happy the show was over, and I felt a giant weight lift from my shoulders. But I felt like I was kind of going through the motions of my life. *Dance Moms* and the ALDC had been such a huge part of my journey thus far, and it was weird not to have them anymore. For almost a decade, I'd gotten used to a routine that no longer existed.

Complicating matters further, I had no idea what I wanted to do next. I liked being on TV, and I loved the performing arts, so I knew I wanted to remain in the entertainment business, but I didn't want to be a backup dancer. I felt like I had done that my whole life. I also no longer had the option of reverting to being just an ordinary girl from Pittsburgh. I no longer knew what it was like to live a normal life. How was I going to blend in when everyone knew my name wherever I went? Having people stare at me who knew my history and backstory was a little weird. I also wasn't sure how I would be able to juggle classes and upcoming gigs. I was overwhelmed because this massive space in my life that used to be filled was now an empty, dark hole. I felt lost and unsure of what came next. Where did I fit in?

Dancing for Myself

I used to look forward to dancing every day. I'd given my life to perfecting my craft, but I no longer had a healthy relationship with it. Instead, it made me sad and anxious. I felt like no matter how good I got, I was always going to be seen as the girl at the bottom of the pyramid. I posted dance videos on my YouTube channel, but not everyone who watched the show watched them. Everyone in the dance world knew me, which meant I couldn't just walk into a dance studio without the fear of being recorded and scrutinized because I had been on TV. I was in this weird zone where I felt like people saw me as a washed-up competitive dancer but also experienced in the entertainment industry. I worried that I was never going to prove myself as a dancer, that Abby had destroyed my dance reputation.

I'd watch videos online that featured amazing dancers in various dance classes, and a part of me would think, *Oh, I really want to do those classes!* But I was too scared to set foot in another studio. I hadn't danced in months, and I was nervous to underperform. I couldn't handle being filmed and humiliated. I'd already endured almost a decade of that and would not put myself through it again.

Even now, I am leery about every dance class I go to. I don't want anyone to film me in the wrong way. This apprehension is annoying because I should be able to take a class and have fun and be free to make mistakes. Dance isn't always a perfect expression, especially in class. Missteps happen. But I felt like I had to be flawless, otherwise I'd be judged. And then people would just continue to believe what Abby had said all along.

I did, however, consider giving dance another go when some of the moms from the last season approached me and my mom wanting to put together a tour. We would travel to different cities around the world and perform new dances and do meet and greets. The girls included myself, Kalani, Kendall, and Chloé, who had returned during season 7. The project was called the Irreplaceables Tour, and it would be arranged by our moms, our respective management, and a tour company. The idea was promising, but the organization of the event was all over the place. Management thought it was up to our moms to handle all the coordination, and our moms were looking to the tour company to do the work. Even though we had begun practicing for the event, we never signed a contract because there were so many questions from my legal team. My brothers also did not love the idea of my mom traveling again. They had just gotten her back after several years of having her on the road with me filming *Dance Moms*. With this in mind, we made the decision not to participate in the tour.

When we pulled out, Kira, Kalani's mom, sent us an email threatening to sue my mom and me, so we had to get legal counsel. Luckily, she had no legal standing. Despite pulling out, I lost a great friend—Camryn—over the tour because I did not share with her that it was being put together. In this industry you're taught not to say anything until legal contracts have been signed, and since nothing was agreed to, I never mentioned it to her. The whole situation was a mess and put a strain on my relationships with the other girls as well, but I felt especially bad because Camryn was hurt that I had kept it from her, especially since she was not included in the lineup.

Though I chose not to participate, the tour continued on, and it would be years before I got my friends back. Camryn and I have since rekindled our relationship, but I felt horribly about how everything went down. I never wanted anyone to get hurt.

I had lived a somewhat sheltered life because of the show and how busy I was with dance. I was with my mom 24–7, so it wasn't like I was like out there partying and hanging out. I didn't have a lot of interactions with other people my age, nor did I have a good barometer of what a healthy relationship was, friendship or otherwise. Figuring out what true friendship meant to me, what my relationship to authority figures was going to be, and what a romantic relationship should offer was challenging. I had been conditioned by my experiences on *Dance Moms* to be a people pleaser. Of course, I failed miserably despite my best efforts. My being at the bottom of the pyramid was a clear indication to me that people were in fact *not* pleased with me. Sometimes Abby couldn't even remember why I was at the bottom; it seemed like she was just used to seeing me there, so that was a good enough reason. I embraced bad habits and seemed drawn to people who, although charismatic, were exceptional at sucking the joy out of me. I was looking for love and acceptance in all the wrong places.

I confided in my mom, and she turned to someone who had helped me a great deal in the past: Stacy Kaiser, the child therapist from the show. Mom told her that I wasn't doing well since the show had ended a year prior, and that I needed help adjusting.

Stacy listened and comforted me as I told her what I had been through since we had last spoken. She taught me things I had never learned about or even thought of before. She told me that I was an empath, someone who is highly in tune with others' emotions. I know people make light of it and don't take it seriously, but being an empath can cause serious emotional harm to the person constantly taking on other people's feelings and problems. She remembered how I would get upset anytime the girls on the show were yelled at. I cared deeply.

She then went on to tell me what a narcissist was, someone who is "extremely resistant to changing their behavior, even when it's causing them problems. Their tendency is to turn the blame on others."[1] This definition made me think of Abby. As she spoke, I wondered why Stacy hadn't told me this years ago, when I was still on the show. But then I realized I'd been just a kid—I didn't have the capacity to handle such big feelings. Plus, back then I was still in the situation. It's hard to reflect on an experience while living it.

Our discussions emphasized protecting my heart. I was so used to people taking their anger out on me. Even though it sounded simple, I had no idea how to protect myself. I had to start being intentional about who I let into my life and take more control over who I let get close to me. If someone wasn't adding value, then I needed to minimize my time with them or remove them altogether.

Stacy also brought up all the times I would hide in the bathroom and cry when I was hurt. She reminded me that showing emotion was okay, that humans are supposed to cry. And she was right. I never wanted to let people know how they affected me, that I was vulnerable and could be hurt, because I knew they would use it against me. As a way to protect myself, I hid my feelings by isolating when I got overwhelmed. Then I'd return unfazed . . . or so I thought. I didn't realize that I was still getting hurt in the process. This behavior ultimately showcased how much I lacked confidence and self-assurance, steadily looking for validation in others instead of looking within myself. I felt like I couldn't do anything right, that I wasn't good enough.

I had a long way to go to heal emotionally, but the first step of that journey was learning how to set boundaries and not let others take advantage of me. I would no longer allow my heavy emotional burdens to weigh me down. The bad habits would take some effort to unlearn, but I had never been a quitter and would not stop now. My mental health was just as important as my physical health, and I only wanted to feel better.

Over time I learned that if I got a funny feeling about someone, I should trust my gut and proceed with caution or steer clear of them. I was starting to understand that if I didn't like someone or didn't want to do something, I didn't have to—and that was okay. As long as I was happy and not hurting anyone in the process, I got to do what I wanted.

One of Stacy's statements that continues to ring true to me is that no one has the right to make you feel bad about yourself. If someone does make me feel this way, I need to limit my interactions with them. This can be difficult when the person in question is someone you have grown up with. For a people pleaser who hates confrontation, this was hard for me, and it took a while to get the hang of it. I stopped texting, calling, hanging out, and being available to those people who emptied my cup. Initially, I felt lousy after setting these boundaries. A few times I reminded myself why I liked hanging out with someone, only to rediscover why I needed to cut back my time with them. I recognized who I had to make a clean break from, and though I used to feel guilty about it, I don't anymore. I love myself too much.

As I uncovered these truths, I had to do some serious soul-searching. In order to stop allowing toxic people into my life and making excuses for them, I needed to figure out how I wanted to be treated. In the past, I would let people say or do whatever, not wanting to cause waves if I spoke up or stood up for myself. That wasn't going to be my approach going forward.

My healing journey is part of the reason why I decided to write this book. For a long time, I was too afraid to tell my side of things because I was broken and unsure of how people would perceive me. However, with the work I've done on myself, I feel like I can finally let go and have the guts to talk about my experiences. My intention isn't to make anyone look bad. But I do believe that in order to move away from my past, I have to acknowledge it. I can't avoid things that hurt me because that pain will root itself deep inside me and fester. True healing requires that I get comfortable with my own story, my wins and losses, the pretty and the ugly, and explore new ways to move forward.

When *Dance Moms* ended, I had a lot of work to do on myself, which took a long time. With effort and support, little by little, I recognized which people were not my friends and did not love me. I was used to going above and beyond, bending myself in half to make everyone else happy. But after years of bending, I was starting to break. Those who love you do not hurt you and take advantage of you to benefit themselves. Instead, they strive to make your life easier, better, and more fulfilled. I had to refocus my energy and remove the negative people from my life to get to a better, healthier me. The one whose position at the bottom of the pyramid did not make her a victim but instead made her stronger.

One of the best things to come out of my *Dance Moms* experience was that it normalized the importance of therapy. I am not sure what that says about the show, but I will say it was beneficial to have a therapist on set. Stacy helped me understand the complexities of working with certain individuals. She also provided some excellent coping skills, resources, and strategies that have served me well. I saw the benefits of working with her, which is why I am so passionate about projects that support mental health. I have *Dance Moms* to thank for giving me a reason to work with a therapist while at the same time providing a therapist for me to work with.

Over time, I built myself back up. Surrounding myself with family definitely helped. It was a period of growth when I got to learn what I actually wanted—not only for my career but for my life.

A little more than a year after I left the show, I got a call from Chloe and Maud inviting me to meet them at GRANVILLE for dinner. My mom and I were in LA, and we were excited to hang out with them. Chloe and Maud had become great mentors for me. We'd get together every once in a while when we happened to be in the same place. They were bicoastal, in LA and New York, so they were always traveling for work. I had just gone through a bad breakup, and by this point, I had stopped dancing completely. I wasn't planning to return to dance ever again.

As we were catching up, they asked if I was taking classes. I told them no; I wasn't dancing anymore because I knew I didn't want to be a professional dancer. I felt that no one would want to hire me anyway, because Abby had tarnished my reputation. I wanted to focus on music and acting.

Their expressions spoke volumes as I continued explaining myself. They were looking at me as if I was speaking gibberish.

It felt good to talk about dance with people who were successful in the dance industry. Chloe and Maud knew me, and they knew my abilities. It was clear to them that I was burned out and discouraged, but they recognized that I had talent. Although they were not judging me, they were shocked by my lack of motivation. I was a shell of the Nia they had first met. I guess I was a pretty sad sight.

They quickly went into action. Before I knew it, we were making a plan for private dance classes. They reminded me that I was a dancer at my core, and no one could take that away. They were concerned that I had lost my spark and were determined to reignite it before the flame was snuffed out completely. They reminded me that we all knew people who used to dance and had quit. No one ever said they were happy they quit dance, but we'd heard plenty of people express regret that they hadn't kept dancing.

That was what I needed to hear. Our conversation resonated with me and got me thinking. Was I ready to give up on dance? Was all that time I had invested in dancing done in vain? Would I be mad or disappointed in myself if I stopped dancing? Most importantly, Chloe and Maud reminded me that I was a dancer first. I could pursue all sorts of other paths in entertainment, but my foundation in the arts would always be dance.

Chloe and Maud stuck to their word and set up privates for me with a few of their dance instructor friends. These were one-on-one sessions, so I felt a little less self-conscious, but I was seriously overthinking everything. I was timid and afraid to let loose and let my guard down. For so long I had been told I wasn't a good dancer, and now that I hadn't been practicing or taking classes, I was that much harder on myself. I felt like I had lost my pizzazz; I had no enthusiasm or attitude anymore. My inner Sasha Fierce was nowhere to be found. However, with each class, I started to feel better.

Once I got back to taking privates with Chloe and Maud's friends, I filmed my sessions but didn't post them. To be honest, I'm still really nervous about posting dance videos. I'm sure one day I'll get the courage to do it, but for now I love having dance all to myself. It takes the pressure off a bit.

I am so thankful to people like Chloe and Maud. Without them, I probably would have stopped dancing after the show ended. I am blessed to have so many inspiring people in my corner and grateful to have maintained those relationships. Those connections helped me learn to love dance again—and love myself more completely.

Life After *Dance Moms*

Sometimes the most amazing experiences emerge from the most unexpected places. After the show, I immersed myself in content creation on social media. I wasn't looking to become an influencer; I was just creating content for fun. Social media provided an outlet for me to use my voice and be myself—a huge relief, having come from a situation where I was always on edge.

As my following exploded, I was invited by Musical.ly to be a social media correspondent for them and NBC at the 2018 Winter Olympics in South Korea. I also worked with the tourism board of Australia and went to the UK to promote *Just Dance* live. Social media had been just fun when I started, but now it was opening the door to breathtaking opportunities. I was traveling the world, working with brands, even sitting on panels and public speaking.

I had goals after I left the show, and I was checking them off one by one. I did not want to be a one-hit wonder, and I worried that my success would be limited to my experience on *Dance Moms*. Social media allowed me to leverage every opportunity I had because I knew there was more to my career than being at the bottom of the pyramid. Now everyone had a chance to see that too.

Since I'd been traveling back and forth to LA for various opportunities, I ended up attending high school virtually at PA Cyber School, studying there from the second part of my sophomore year until I graduated. My desire was to get an apartment in LA; I thought living there full-time would be the perfect way to explore opportunities in entertainment.

When I told my father this, though, he snapped me back to reality. "If you get a job, you can move to LA," he said. "We just can't afford to move you there." And while I was passionate, he was right. I was sixteen years old and was in no way capable of living across the country without any kind of plan. I also don't think my dad expected me to book anything quickly because I was still relatively green and hadn't had a lot of experience in the acting world. Plus, he finally had me home more since I'd fulfilled the *Dance Moms* contract, and he was excited to spend more time with me.

But I wasn't thinking of any of that. I was thinking of how I could make my move happen. So, I decided, *Okay. It's game time now.*

Because he hadn't said no.

He'd just said I needed a job first. I was a girl on a mission.

I was soon presented with another chance of a lifetime. I signed with my first big talent advisory company, United Talent Agency. UTA represents a vast number of celebrities for TV, film, books, and more, so signing with them was a huge step in my career. Soon after the ink was dried on the agreement, I was sent on an audition for a soap opera called *The Bold and the Beautiful.*

I had a great audition, and they ended up booking me for the show. I would play the character of Emma, who was given a really cool storyline. She was a fashion intern at Forrester Creations, brought in to work on the relaunch of the Hope for the Future Campaign. Emma had to navigate the world of money, high fashion, and love, all while staying true to herself and her budding career. I was a little nervous when I did the read. This was new territory, and I'd never done a scripted show like this before.

Booking a scripted series after being on reality TV was a big deal. I could now say I was an actress on a network television show. My family was so excited for me and encouraged me to take the job. This kind of opportunity was what I had been working toward.

Initially, I was only supposed to have a guest appearance on the show, but a few episodes turned into me becoming a series regular. Since the show was filmed in LA, I finally was able to get an apartment there. A month after that conversation with my dad, I had found a job. He was shocked but extremely happy for me. I couldn't believe I'd be living in LA full-time at just sixteen years old. My age also meant I had to have a parent or guardian on set. I was not emancipated, so my mom moved with me and accompanied me to filming.

Because I was paying for the residence, my mom gave me a lot of ownership on where we would rent our first home. We found a beautiful townhome in Glendale, which gave me a fresh start from our days living in West Hollywood for *Dance Moms*. I was in a new community, providing me a space to grow. My commute to work was not bad, and my mom would drive me so I had extra time to run lines or nap in the car. My dad and brothers came out to visit me when they could. Considering my roots were in Pittsburgh, I made sure to spend time there when I was not working. I was officially bicoastal, and I loved it.

The Bold and the Beautiful was the best learning experience for me. I discovered so much about myself and about acting. I got to work each day with amazing people who were veterans in the field. I was nervous each time I stepped on set because there was a lot of dialogue to learn in a short period of time. We received the scripts only a few days in advance, which often meant our lines were changing even as we began to film. It reminded me of competing in dance. We learned so many routines each week and had to perfect them in a short time span, so this experience was flexing a similar mental muscle.

Filming two episodes a day was challenging, but the complex schedule prepared me as an actress. It challenged me to get into character at the drop of a dime. The cast was fantastic and also a huge help on my learning curve. They were patient with me as I navigated this unfamiliar space and gave me tools to help with line memorization and calming my nerves. When I started, the show was celebrating its thirty-first anniversary, so the energy was top-tier. It amazed me that the show had been on for almost twice as long as I had been alive. I had the pleasure of working with some of the people who had been cast members from the very beginning. I learned a lot watching how they practiced and performed. I remember the director also taught me how to do the famous "soap opera look." You know, the one whenever you see the person at the end of a scene and they're staring off into the distance while holding a straight face.

I also loved that the show was conscientious of my dialogue, makeup, costumes, and character choices, considering I was under eighteen. Hair and makeup were fun experiences. I even started experimenting with wigs to make it easier to get ready and also protect my hair.

The actor who played my love interest was a gentleman and easy to work with. We had several scenes where we had to kiss, hug, or touch, but everyone remained professional. I had never done something quite like that before, so they would always make sure I was comfortable. If I didn't want to do something, they were totally fine with it. They took my lead on how much or how little we would interact.

Our scenes together were actually quite mechanical, and there was nothing romantic about any kiss or other intimacy we shared, though it definitely looked the opposite on camera. I had done some acting before, including kissing, so it wasn't like this was my first on-screen kiss. But in order to have a scene fade out to commercial, we'd have to maintain what we were doing at the end of the scene for an extended period of time. The act of holding a kiss for a long time was quite funny. Likewise, holding eye contact or looking into the distance while we waited for the camera to cut could be intense, especially dependent on the context of the scene.

I was one of the youngest cast members for a bit, but then I was pleased when another girl my age joined the cast. Maile Brady, Wayne Brady's daughter, played my best friend on the show, and we became good friends in real life too. I loved having someone I could relate to on set. We still maintain a great friendship.

Another special moment for me while I was on *B&B* was that I had the opportunity to attend the Daytime Emmy Awards. I also got a prenomination for a Daytime Emmy. I didn't even know that was a thing, but it was surreal to see how close I was to getting an Emmy nomination. It was so amazing to see my cast members up onstage accepting awards for their work. I couldn't believe I got to work with Emmy Award winners and on a show that had won so many Emmys. It felt like I was on my way to accomplishing my dream of being an EGOT—someone who wins an Emmy, a Grammy, an Oscar, and a Tony.

I worked on *The Bold and the Beautiful* for two amazing seasons before my character, unfortunately, died. Getting killed off the show was bittersweet because my departure was abrupt and unexpected. I was just thankful to have had an iconic death. Emma had gotten ahold of some important information and was driving to reveal the secret she had learned when someone texted her. As she looked down to respond to the text, she drove off a cliff and perished, thus bringing an end of my days on *The Bold and the Beautiful*. At least I went out with a bang! I was told the ratings for those episodes were extremely high, so it felt good knowing I had left an impact.

Though my time on the show was short, people still remember my character. During a trip to Australia, I discovered *The Bold and the Beautiful* was just as popular there as *Dance Moms*, so I was recognized for both shows while visiting.

After my departure, the show aired some of my scenes as flashbacks before I was faded out completely. But hey, you never know—no one ever truly dies on a soap opera. You can always come back from the dead or return as a ghost or as someone's evil twin sister. Maybe you'll see me on there again one day.

With *The Bold and the Beautiful* in my rearview mirror, I had to figure out what came next. At the time I had not even thought of college because I loved acting and performing and wanted to do more of that. I began taking any opportunity I could get because I was curious and trying to find what stuck. Dancing was no longer a part of my daily, or sometimes even my weekly, routine, so I needed to fill my time with other things. Although I felt more confident in my dancing, I still had this voice in the back of my head saying I wasn't good enough.

Since I no longer had a full-time gig, I traveled back and forth between Pittsburgh and LA during my final year of high school. I loved the opportunity to reconnect with friends and extended family. It felt good to be a teenager and do teenage things, like going to games with my cousin and brothers and hanging out at dinners and parties. I also continued dancing for myself and striving to learn more about what brought me joy. I was excited to rediscover the person I'd lost.

As time drew near to begin applying for college, I started feeling anxious. This decision was a move into adulthood that would have a major impact on my future, and I was overthinking every step of the process for fear I would not make the right choice. While researching colleges and universities around the country, I kept thinking, *Is this the right thing to do? What do I want to study? Is college even for me? Will college stunt my growth in the entertainment industry? Should I just stop now and jump straight into a career? And if so, what career? Acting? Music? Dance?* I was at a crossroads with no clear path forward.

Yet there was something about LA I couldn't shy away from. I always saw myself living on the West Coast and didn't want to let my past hardships dictate my future. One thing was certain: My mom was moving back to Pittsburgh because I was now eighteen. During this time of testing being in LA by myself, I called my mom constantly, confiding in her how much I was stressing out about the college application process and the decisions that lay ahead of me. I was so overwhelmed that Mom suggested I finish whatever applications I'd already started and just take a gap year to figure things out. That plan made sense, so I finished up my applications to a few UC schools, including UCLA. I was excited about applying there because I had done an event on UCLA's campus the year before, working with Michelle Obama's Reach Higher program.

The opportunity had come to me by way of Todd Krim, with whom I'd worked on some volunteer projects in the past. He was involved with a number of charities and community projects and reached out to me to see if I had any interest in this one. My yes was automatic. Todd connected me with the Reach Higher team, and through my participation in that event as a junior in high school, I was introduced to the world of voter advocacy. Although that Reach Higher event was focused on the celebration of college signing day, there were also members of Civic Nation, now called When We All Vote, present. When We All Vote is a bipartisan organization that focuses on voter education and resources. WWAV and Reach Higher are both organizations founded by Michelle Obama. Although the missions of the organizations are distinct, there was a great deal of overlap with my interests because I was part of the targeted demographic. I was thrilled to get involved.

These organizations helped me learn the importance of making contacts in a variety of opportunities because you never know when these relationships may intersect or connect. I didn't go into these experiences with an agenda but with an open mind. They have provided so many rich and rewarding projects and relationships for the future.

Despite having visited several college campuses over the years, I had never felt any particular connection to the schools. That all changed when I visited UCLA. For the first time, I could see myself on a college campus and thriving. This feeling took me by surprise. Reflecting on that day, I was happy to send off the application. I had also considered Carnegie Mellon because they had a fantastic theater program, and after my time off-Broadway, I wanted to do more of that. After a college visit there—and discovering I'd missed the application deadline to apply—I pretty much went about my regular life.

With my mom gone, I decided to downsize my residence, since I was still trying to figure out what to do after graduation. I found a roommate, a friend I had made during one of my theatrical experiences, to share an apartment with. That was a great relief to my parents because they didn't have to worry about me living on my own in LA. My parents helped me move in with my new roommate in March 2020, the weekend before the world shut down at the beginning of the COVID-19 pandemic. Then I went home to Pittsburgh with my parents. Little did I know it would be several months before I lived full-time in this apartment; once the shutdown happened, work dried up and there was no need to be in LA, so I stayed in Pittsburgh with my family.

I felt a profound sense of relief putting the process on hold while I focused on enjoying my senior year and working. Still, in the back of my mind, I worried about the details of my application, like not having the right grades or experience to be admitted anywhere, since I had been homeschooled for most of my secondary education. Yes, I'd been in honors programs, but I didn't take many of the exams that regular-track high school students take. I was at a disadvantage and didn't have a ton of advanced-level credits. My one saving grace was my strong GPA and my résumé of community activities.

But I did my best to let go of all these concerns and lean into the gap year my mom had suggested. It would allow me the space to think about what I wanted to do without the added pressure of college. Then the COVID-19 pandemic hit, and the life I wanted so badly for myself seemed to once again slip through my grasp.

The one positive thing that came out of this time was that it forced my family to slow down and stay in one place. Since productions had shut down and there was no work in LA, I remained in Pittsburgh, and for months, we got to enjoy one another's company like we used to do when I was a kid. This was the longest I had been home since I was nine years old. We played games, watched movies, cooked, and shared meals together. I felt like a child again, with no cares in the world. This was a special time for my parents, too, because they got to have all their kids in one place for a while, something we hadn't been able to do since we were always so busy and on the go.

This time of reflection and healing was what my spirit needed before figuring out where and if I was going to attend college. I was slowly learning how to define success for myself and protect my peace.

One evening, as my family sat down to have dinner, the status of my college applications came up in conversation because people online were posting about getting into colleges. This reminded my mom of my pending applications. "Hey, did you ever hear back from UCLA?"

I honestly hadn't checked my email in a couple of days, so I wasn't sure. "Oh, I don't know," I said before reaching for my cell phone and opening my inbox. Sure enough, there was an unread email from UCLA. I opened it without a second thought.

My eyes quickly scanned the contents of the email. "I think I got in?" I said.

My brothers were the first to comment. EJ said, "No way!" smiling from ear to ear.

I passed my phone to my mom to look at the email, and she confirmed it. "Yeah, you got in!"

I think everyone was shocked. My brothers didn't believe it, so I had to pass my phone around the table to make sure everyone saw the same thing I was seeing. I couldn't believe it either. Everyone congratulated me and told me how proud they were of me. *I got into UCLA!* This was such a huge accomplishment. My entire family understood what a big deal this was, particularly my brother EJ. He had looked up the stats and requirements to get into the school and recognized that my acceptance was no easy feat. UCLA is difficult to get into, only accepting about 9 percent of its applicants.[1]

Since the whole world had shut down because of COVID and everything was up in the air, I decided to pivot my plans and enroll in college. I'm a firm believer in everything happening for a reason, and timing was key. Once the news reached my whole family, my nana called to make sure I was going to commit to UCLA. She didn't give me a choice—she told me I was going!

This was just another example of life taking an unexpected turn. I was beginning to learn that things always have a funny way of working out.

To celebrate my acceptance, my mom bought a cake from Giant Eagle, the local grocery store in Pittsburgh. Their cakes are so yummy. I put on the UCLA T-shirt I'd bought during the event I'd attended the year prior, and we took pictures. I felt like my having the shirt was a sign of what was to come, though this possibility hadn't been on my mind when I bought it. We celebrated at the house as a family, and their eagerness and support made me even more excited. I couldn't wait to head back out to LA.

During my freshman year, I was hoping to live on campus, but unfortunately, the entire year was held online due to the pandemic. I was sad that I would have to be cyberschooled for another year, but it ended up being a blessing in disguise. Not only did it help me adjust to the college workload from being homeschooled for so long, but I also booked a movie called *Imperfect High* and was able fly to Vancouver, Canada, to film the project, though I couldn't bring anyone with me because of the pandemic.

The COVID protocols were strict, and everyone was on high alert for any sign of illness. When I arrived, I had to quarantine in my hotel room for two weeks before we began filming. We were on set for three weeks. That was the first time I was on a project for such a long period of time alone. It was a little unnerving, considering there was a global health crisis taking place around me. I didn't want to make a mistake and get locked up because Canada's COVID rules were strict. If you were caught breaking their pandemic regulations, you could get fined or worse.

Still, I had a great time working on the movie. I was stoked that I got to star in a feature film. *Imperfect High* is the sequel to a film called *Perfect High*, which released in 2015. My character, Hanna, suffered from an anxiety disorder and fell into the wrong friend group, which led to her drug abuse. This caused issues between Hanna and her mom, Deborah—played by Sherri Shepherd—as Deborah tried to navigate her child through some dangerous situations.

Sherri Shepherd is so lovely and talented at what she does. I learned a lot from her, and we established a bond on- and off-screen. She taught me various tools as an actress and even gifted me an acting workbook and a handwritten note our last day of filming. Her genuine and humble spirit was just what I needed to get me through my first lead role in a film. The cherry on top was that the movie did really well for the network.

Another of my accomplishments from that time was writing a children's book called *Today I Dance*, which was published in

2020. It's about a little girl going into her first dance class and learning how to dance. It captures the excitement I felt when I was young. The best part is the cover image, which features a dancer who looks just like me.

I was moving on to a new phase of my life, and my opportunities to continue making an impact were evolving along with me.

College Years

Voting has always been important in my household. My parents would go early before work, and we'd travel together as a family to the voting booths. My brothers and I would watch as both our parents executed their right to democracy. As soon as I turned eighteen, I made sure to register to vote. Voting is even more crucial now than it was back then. I am giddy whenever organizations reach out for my help in spreading the word.

During my freshman year of college, I became more involved in voter advocacy. The Civic Nation program hosted the first major voting event I was a part of, but it certainly wasn't the last. Michelle Obama's team asked me if I wanted to continue working on various voter programs, and I was thrilled. I had been doing videos on my social media about how voting works and why it's so important, so this was special to me, especially since I was approaching my first year as an eligible voter.

I found a variety of ways to volunteer. I enjoyed working at a voter registration and food drive at Heinz Field in Pittsburgh. One of the people I met was Jade Bernad, who worked for Civic Nation. Jade took me under her wing and became a mentor to me. She taught me how to navigate the political world as a woman of color—how to carry myself, remain passionate about my initiatives, stay involved, and position myself with the right people to make things happen. She was innovative and loved helping people as well. Having the chance to talk with her and seeing where I fit into all these opportunities, where I could be doing more, reminded me why it was so important that I use my platform to stand for what I believe in. I am proud of my efforts and the difference I made in my community.

Everyone worked tirelessly in southwest Pennsylvania to increase voter turnout, and we saw the results of our efforts. We had significant participation of young voters in the 2020 election, and those numbers were essential in swinging the vote. I can look back and say I was part of something much bigger than me. This was the beginning of my advocacy work, and I loved it.

After that, more organizations reached out for similar assistance—groups like I Am a Voter and I Will Vote. I got more heavily involved in other issues I felt passionate about, specifically with the Democratic National Convention (DNC). I got to interview Senator Edward Markey, Pennsylvania governor Josh Shapiro, and Dr. Anthony Fauci, the former chief medical advisor to the president.

From there, I was plugged into various political organizations and eventually people who worked at the White House on other topics, like providing resources for COVID care and fighting for women's rights. My relationship with the DNC led to the First Lady, Dr. Jill Biden, inviting me to the White House for their annual holiday decorations celebration. I knew it was a big deal as soon as I received the invitation. I was honored, especially because the list of attendees was so limited due to the pandemic. The small group of influencers I was included in was told there was a strict protocol with masks and COVID testing. I didn't care about all of that—I was going to the White House!

I had never been there before and had no idea if I'd ever be going back, so I knew I wanted to make a statement. I splurged and purchased my first real designer suit, a Chanel, along with my first pair of Louboutin heels. I also made sure to take a ton of photos. I ended up being invited to the next three holiday events as well, and even met Dr. Biden herself. I had no idea that first visit would lead to a long-standing relationship with the White House and the DNC.

The world was finally returning to some sort of normalcy, so for my sophomore year, I would begin taking in-person classes on the UCLA campus. My parents encouraged me to live on campus because they wanted me to have the full college experience. I would still keep my apartment, so if I hated dorm life, I had an escape that wasn't far away. It was a luxury I was willing to pay for because I valued my privacy. I also had little experience being in a traditional school environment. It had been years since I was in school with other students, let alone living with other people. I had never shared a room before. The whole concept was a bit scary and intimidating. I did love the idea of decorating a dorm room and having suitemates, though, and I agreed with my parents that this was an important part of college life that would help me learn how to become an adult. There were so many life skills I still had to learn that have nothing to do with books or studying.

While on campus, I discovered that UCLA had a student-led dance club called Icarus Contemporary. I decided to audition and was chosen for the team. I rehearsed two or three times a week and even performed at basketball games, UCLA events, and social gatherings around campus. Though we didn't compete, I adored being onstage again. The dancers there were so talented, and having the ability to share my love of dance with them was another step in my journey to healing.

I was excited to discover that if you wanted to choreograph for Icarus, there were several opportunities to do so—whether it was just a combination for class or an entire piece for small groups, trios, duets, or solos. We would perform as a group for big events, but for the end-of-year showcase, we got to perform the dances we choreographed. I had never thought about choreographing before, but this encouraged me to try a new lane that I wanted to explore further. I discovered that I actually loved choreographing.

My junior year, I did a big push for the midterm elections and went to Washington, DC, to meet with the DNC, along with other influencers involved in voter advocacy. The midterm elections have an incredible impact on voters' lives, both locally and regionally. I wanted to use my platform in a productive way and was excited to help with voter education and encouraging young people to vote. During my visit, I got to go into the press room and watch President Biden give a speech on the importance of the COVID vaccine and booster shot. And then the most amazing thing happened: I got to meet him.

At the conclusion of his speech, the other influencers and I were led outside, and after we'd waited a few minutes, the president of the United States came out to meet us and took a group photo with us on the steps. Our impromptu meet and greet was spectacular, but it didn't end there. President Biden proceeded to invite us into the Oval Office, a private section of the White House where only restricted government personnel are allowed to enter. I was in awe. The blue carpet, the flags, the beautifully crafted wooden desk, the staff buzzing around . . . It was surreal. We spent an hour touring the Oval Office, and President Biden spoke casually as he directed us into some of his private offices within the suite. There is one grand room with other rooms branching off it. We went into a meeting room that had several pictures of his family and friends. He showed us awards and gifts that he had been given throughout his political career and explained the importance of each keepsake.

When we returned to the Oval Office, he said, "You guys are really young, yet you have a huge platform. Use it for good. You could be our next world leaders." He was thoroughly impressed by us content creators and told us about the power of influence and how we can and should use our platforms for positive change, to inspire people. "Any one of you could be president one day."

I was floored! I could not believe the POTUS was telling me that I could one day be standing in his shoes. It was special because for just a moment, he was a regular guy sharing his memories with us. It made him more personable, human.

On our way out of the facility, I got to meet Dr. Fauci in person, which was amazing after having interviewed him virtually. I also met the surgeon general, Vivek Murthy. That visit was one of the most amazing experiences in DC I've ever had.

Just a few months later, I was invited to see vice president Kamala Harris speak at the University of Michigan. I was the only media correspondent allowed to interview her. Her team had seen the interviews I'd done in the past and approved me. It was cool watching them set up the room in preparation for her talk. The event covered advances in technology and how they were affecting climate change. Vice President Harris was promoting clean-air initiatives for buses, fossil fuels, factories, and the like. I had the opportunity to talk to her about it and why people should be concerned about climate change. I was stunned when I discovered she'd done her research on me as well and was familiar with my advocacy work and what I had been doing with the DNC.

A year later, I did a roundtable event with Vice President Harris, where we discussed reproductive rights, women's rights, and human rights. The focus was on what we can do to maintain a woman's right to make her own health-care decisions and how we can spread the word. My mom and I were seated next to each other at a huge table in Harris's office. Harris came into the room and went around the table greeting everyone and shaking their hands. When she got to me, she said, "It's been a while since I've seen you!" She remembered me from the year prior. I was beyond flattered.

She sat down next to us, at the head of the table, and began her talk. I got to ask questions about her work and how young people can support her. So often the youth are silenced, or they don't necessarily have a say in what happens around them. People think we don't know anything because we're young, which maybe is a little true, but we're trying to learn. "Don't let anyone take your voice and tell you that you can't do something or that you can't have a say in something," she said, stressing the importance of young voters. After the discussion, she and her husband spent time speaking with all of us in attendance.

On my Instagram I used to do something called Role Model Mondays. Each Monday, I would feature someone I looked up to who'd made a difference and highlight how amazing they are. Just ordinary people doing extraordinary things. My followers loved it, which is what led me to produce my first show in 2021, a Facebook Watch series called *Dance with Nia.* I interviewed dancers with disabilities, and then we did a dance routine together. It was beautiful because they got to tell their story through their own lens. I didn't want it to be forced or to make it into something it wasn't. I wanted viewers to see the resilience, effort, and drive of these dancers—not sob stories for views and likes. My focus was that they were comfortable and had control over their stories. It was inspiring to hear of their challenges and how they overcame those obstacles. While *Dance with Nia* was, at its most basic level, about dancers with disabilities, the thing I wanted to highlight was that they were dancers at their core. I hoped this message reaffirmed that dancers come in all different shapes and sizes and bodies.

Alongside my passion projects, I was able to work with some incredible brands, which resulted in one of my biggest personal achievements: I was able to pay my way through school. Having the ability to afford college without putting a financial strain on my family was important to me and something I had planned for. I didn't want to burden my family with paying for my education. Part of the reason I was able to pay for school without taking out student loans is because of my amazing agents. I told them my goal of graduating from college with no debt, and they kept me working consistently to make that happen. I am incredibly grateful for the opportunities they provided me. My schedule was hectic and required some juggling, but I pulled it off.

My senior year I became a member of Alpha Kappa Alpha Sorority, Incorporated. My mother is an AKA as well, so this was significant for the two of us. Though UCLA had not had a line (a new intake for the chapter) in years, I was thankful they welcomed the AKAs back to campus before I graduated. Being surrounded by like-minded Black women was just what my spirit needed. Building a sisterhood and getting to know the women on my line and within the AKA organization was a blessing. I found true friends—sisters—for life.

Attending college was the best decision I ever made. It taught me about life, about myself, and about my relationship with others. I discovered how to deal with tough situations and how to manage a chaotic schedule all on my own. It taught me an independence I likely would not have gained otherwise. I thoroughly enjoyed my classes and hearing the variety of perspectives from students and educators alike. I explored electives that, while challenging, grew my mind in ways I couldn't have imagined.

In 2024 I directed my first campaign with Ad Council, which is a pretty big deal. Ad Council is an organization whose mission is to "convene the best storytellers to educate, unite and uplift—by opening hearts, inspiring action and accelerating change."[1] The campaign I worked on was about mental health, specifically in young adults. I did a session called "Capture the Convo," where I had candid conversations about mental health. I brought together about five or six of my friends who are also in the entertainment business, and we all spoke about our experiences. I worked with mental health experts on how to best approach the sensitive topics we covered, like suicidal thoughts, anxiety, and depression.

Without going through what I went through at the ALDC, I would never have paved my own path, which led me to working with Vice President Kamala Harris, President Joe Biden, and the former Obama administration. What began as a passion of mine—voter registration—transformed into an accomplishment I couldn't have dreamed of. Vice President Harris's run for president made my time working with her even more spectacular. It reaffirmed that what I am doing is good.

In my apartment, I have framed a multitude of letters from political figures. I have a letter from President Joe Biden, and I have three from Michelle Obama, all pretty fricking special. And after I became an AKA, Vice President Harris sent me a special correspondence congratulating me, since she is a part of the organization as well. It's extremely cool to be sorority sisters with a vice president! But while it's exciting to meet and work with powerful, important people, what matters most to me is taking what I've learned on my journey and giving back to the community to make it a better place. All I want to do is help people in the way that others did not help me. I am inspired by my parents to create some type of nonprofit organization. I don't have all the details worked out yet, but it's coming.

I can honestly say that I am doing exactly what I want to be doing, and this is only the beginning. There is so much more in store for me. My biggest goal is to continue storytelling through any medium I can. I want to honor others' voices just as much as I've honored my own.

Star in Your Own Life

I'm grateful for my social media following because they have truly helped me embrace myself. Social media has become a huge part of my life. It is literally my job right now, a fun one that I get to do in my comfort zone, which is a blessing. I have loved watching my fan base grow over the years, and I remember a time when I didn't think I'd ever have as large a following as others. How wrong I was.

Years ago Caleb McLaughlin, who plays Lucas on *Stranger Things*, mentioned that he noticed a drastic difference in the number of followers within the show's fandom.[1] I knew instantly what he was talking about. For years I had noticed the same phenomenon in the *Dance Moms* fandom. The show's other cast members had significantly higher follower counts on social media than I did. I'm not complaining; I am so thankful for those who chose to follow me. It's just worth mentioning that I saw it too. My numbers did not reflect my status as the longest-running cast member of the show.

I sometimes look at the followings of others who are on big TV shows and compare their numbers to that of their Black castmates, and I've noticed a pattern: Almost every time, the Black castmates have fewer followers.

I know for some this might seem trite and silly, but when you're in the spotlight and you see others completing milestones just for being conventionally beautiful while you have to work twice as hard, it definitely affects how you think of yourself and your accomplishments. The disparity in earnings of Black creators is a hot topic, as is their limited representation.

I recognize that social media is innately designed for us to compare ourselves with others. I have had to make a conscious effort to focus on using my platform to *tell* my story and not *compare* my story. That comparison trap can be destructive to your ego and psyche. In the community I have created, what makes me happiest is the sense of togetherness we've established. When I accomplish something, I feel the rallying of my followers cheering me on. That is an incredible feeling and a great source of strength. My followers have my back.

I also cannot deny how much social media has opened me up to so many amazing and life-changing opportunities. I began my journey toward self-acceptance on YouTube, and it grew into movies, off-Broadway shows, TV shows, working with some of my favorite brands, and political advocacy. The continued support and love I receive from my online family extends to every facet of my life—as a college student, an actress, an activist, and a dancer.

Remember how Abby criticized my braids for looking like a log coming out of my head? I've been grateful for the support on social media I received as I've chronicled my experiences with wearing my hair natural. Sharing the highs and lows of this journey has made me feel vulnerable, but I wanted people to see me throughout the process. Fans loved that I opened up about the state of my natural hair, and I so appreciated their recommendations of products or protective hairstyles I could use to get it back to its healthy state. I'm glad I didn't allow Abby or anyone else's negative impression of me to linger and ruin my sense of self.

My followers ask me what products I'm using, not just for hair but for makeup, skin care, and even clothing. I feel the love of my internet and virtual aunties, my cheer squad whose comments make me feel seen, valued, and heard. There are people who get me, who understand my journey—perhaps because it is not that uncommon. Many people know what it's like to be the underdog—it's relatable. I share that same grit, passion, and determination with others in the world.

I remember a lot of details from my time on *Dance Moms*. Those were my formative years. They shaped who I am and how I see the world. I interact with people now based on my experiences on the show. Yet as much as I do remember, there are things I have blocked out. Video clips, especially old clips of myself, can trigger unwanted memories. Writing this book forced me to confront some of those. Sorting through the avalanche of emotions took time, and sometimes I needed to step away from my writing, giving myself space to process the feelings.

I marvel at the little girl I used to be. I also marvel at the adults who put her down. Their patterns of continued behavior and verbal vitriol reveal an ugly side to them that I now recognize as an adult. I have the language and understanding of who they truly are and why it was necessary to establish boundaries. I reject the excuse that we were only making a TV show.

During the pandemic, *Dance Moms* had a bit of a revival. A whole new generation was being introduced to the show. Viewers who were not even alive when the show first aired were now watching it. Sound bites from *Dance Moms* became popular on TikTok. There are billions of hits on the app with *Dance Moms* hashtags. The cast of *Dance Moms* was always ready to share their experiences and speak into trending topics. I also discovered that there was a cable channel playing *Dance Moms* nonstop.

The show continues to be incredibly popular despite its controversial elements. Those who grew up watching it now see the show through a different lens. Moments that were originally seen as funny are now considered problematic. Punch lines and storylines are criticized for their racial undertones. Some of the stuff that people used to laugh at is hard to watch. The humor is lost. Yet the show is still filled with magical moments. It is a gem and a force of pop culture that can't be denied. And I was a key part of it. But at what price?

Abby's cancer diagnosis in 2018 sent me into a tailspin of emotions. As much as she'd put me through on and off the show, I never would wish cancer on my worst enemy. She was in and out of the hospital for a while battling the disease.

We had left the ALDC not on the best of terms. It was the right decision, and I have no regrets. However, our abrupt departure left me with no closure from the dance studio I had called home since the age of three. For a decade I danced for Abby, and then one day that was no longer the case.

During the same time Abby was diagnosed with cancer, my acting coach suddenly died from a stroke. I had worked with him for years, and he was instrumental to my growth as an actor. He died right before I booked *The Bold and the Beautiful*. I never had the chance to tell him about booking the role or to thank him for everything he did to get me to that place. It happened fast, and I was left unprepared. On the heels of his death, I heard about Abby's illness, and I did not want the same thing to happen with her. I didn't have a speech prepared, but I wanted to talk to her and let her know how I felt now that I was working in LA. I asked my mom to reach out to see if we could visit Abby. Since we had left the studio under tense circumstances, she contacted Bryan Stinson about helping to coordinate a visit. My mom made it clear that she did not want this visit filmed.

After waiting for some time with no response regarding my checking in on her, Mom eventually shared with me that Abby had denied our hospital visit request—and on my birthday, at that. When I saw the text Abby sent as her response, it was everything I needed to hear to move forward.

In denying our request for a visit, Abby said she'd already heard everything I would have to say from my IG live. She said she was so very proud that I had a script to follow and that she needed to get back to cleaning out her closet, literally and figuratively. Abby then wrote that perhaps Mom was a parent who always thought their child did no wrong and that she wouldn't know because she never saw Mom around me much. If that wasn't enough for me to move on, she concluded by taking credit for getting me out of Pittsburgh, that every penny in my pocket was because of her, and that Mom and I should be grateful to her for not having to shop in thrift stores.

I will never reach out to Abby Lee Miller again. I try my best not to fill my heart with hate, but as far as I'm concerned, she no longer exists in my world, and I like it that way. I wish her no harm; I just want her out of my life. I've even ended relationships with people who keep in contact with her; it's a boundary I've had to set so I can heal.

To be honest, I didn't even want to use her name in this book; just saying it makes me feel like I'm giving her power in my life that she doesn't deserve. But as much as I didn't want to give her attention by naming her, I also didn't want her to be able to hide from the way she treated me. I needed to be explicitly clear about the pain she caused me.

But one thing is for sure: No matter what, I will always remain true to myself and not allow anyone's cruelty or misery to get the best of me. It was on my heart to reach out, and that's what I did. I can only control myself; I cannot control the actions of others.

As for what she said about me, my best response is to continue living in a state of "Don't let anyone steal your joy." I see my joy as an act of resistance. It was the one thing Abby could never control, and that seemed to infuriate her. I think she truly believed that I did not know my place—that she had the right to dictate who got what opportunities and experiences, and by pursuing more for myself, I was ungrateful.

By mid-2020, enough people—both cast and viewers—were calling out Abby's racist behavior that Abby ended up being fired from Lifetime. Although *Dance Moms* had been over for a while, she had been given spin-off shows, which were all canceled. In light of this, she made a public apology on Instagram in June 2020 for how she had behaved on the show:

> I genuinely understand and deeply regret how my words have effected [sic] and hurt those around me in the past, particularly those in the Black community. To Kamryn, Adriana, and anyone else I've hurt, I am truly sorry.
>
> I realize that racism can come not just from hate, but also from ignorance. No matter the cause, it is harmful, and it is my fault. While I cannot change the past or remove the harm I have done, I promise to educate myself, learn, grow, and do better. While I hope to one day earn your forgiveness, I recognize that

> words alone are not enough. I understand it takes time and genuine change.[2]

Though she addressed Kamryn (a dancer from season 8) and her mother, Adriana, the omission of my name spoke volumes to me. It seemed Abby wasn't sorry for how she had treated me. And I was not the only person who took notice—other people called her out on this too. I have yet to receive an apology for anything she has done.

Somehow Abby's pyramid turned into America's pyramid, but at the end of the day, I know those rankings were hers alone. She's one person with one opinion. And I discovered that being at the bottom means you have so much room to grow. If you're always winning and constantly given opportunities, there's always the worry in the back of your head that one day it will stop. The stress of staying at the top is a whole other battle. And if you rush to get to the top, then what? Now you're there, having missed the whole journey—and the journey is what makes you.

I'm grateful that I've been through what I have because it made me appreciate where I'm at every step of the way. Every accomplishment is so much more rewarding when you work for it. The saying "The best view comes from the hardest climb" really is true.

It bothers me sometimes to think that no matter what I have accomplished in my life after *Dance Moms*, I might still be known for being at the bottom of the pyramid. But you know what? I am okay with that. I want people to know that the way others view you does not define you. Of course, I don't want people to see me as weak or a bad dancer, but I also know this book is giving me a chance to reclaim that title and tell my side of the story.

What I have learned most is that, at some point in life, you're going to have obstacles you must overcome. When that happens, I hope you hold on to the truth that you can—and will—overcome them. As long as you still have life to live, you can change your circumstances. People are going to try to steal your joy and tear you down, but you can't let them. You have to decide over and over again that you're not going to let people dim your light and take away your shine. You're going to encounter Abbys in your life, but you can't let them win. Just keep going. You don't have to prove yourself to anyone but you.

When times get hard, I tell myself, *You didn't come this far just to get this far. You still have so much more to do, so much further to go.* I've had people come up to me and ask for a photo and then say, "Who was that really successful girl from the show, though? You know, the one who did really well?" And I just have to let it go, even if it hurts, even if I disagree that I *wasn't* the "really successful" one. Not everyone's going to understand your story, and not everyone's going to care. But even if they don't, you get to know that you are enough and you're doing enough. You are the only one who decides whether you're successful.

Being a Black woman in white spaces sometimes feels like you have to work so much harder to get ahead. If that is you, I hope my story encourages you not to be discouraged or to stop moving toward your goals. Create your own opportunities. Don't wait for someone to choose you. Choose yourself. Understand that you have a right to be there, and you deserve a shot like everyone else.

It doesn't matter how others see you—what matters is how you see yourself and how you choose to move through the world.

I know that when people look at me, they still think of *Dance Moms*. That's fine; the show was a huge part of my life. But now I want you to see past the show and see me for who I really am. A work in progress. A go-getter. Someone who has looked adversity in the face and didn't allow it to dismantle what I know to be true in my heart.

I have done the work. I have learned the lessons. To me, success means coming out on top. It means being true to myself, true to my family, and always keeping God first. I did not go through all this adversity not to succeed. There is a greater purpose for me.

Although I do not go to church every Sunday, I am religious, and I always knew every opportunity, every blessing, was because of God. I also knew that when I was being tested and was at my lowest, He would make a way for me to see things through. That He had a bigger plan for me.

Hard work doesn't always result in an instant win. Sometimes it takes a while, and usually, it takes a lot of soul-searching. But *you* are worth it. *I* am worth it. I have a résumé that's full of amazing experiences. I have a degree on my wall and a book that I wrote. I have a family who loves and supports me, no matter what. I have great friends. So, even if someone has more money than me or more social capital than me, I know I'm still winning in my own right.

At last, I am the star in my own life. And I am ready for whatever comes next.

Acknowledgments

This book has been a long time coming, and there is no possible way I could have executed this project by myself. It truly takes a village.

I want to first thank God because he has given me the strength and vision to tell my story and has blessed me with people who supported and helped me throughout this process.

Thank you to my agents, Melissa and Sam. As soon as I told you both I was ready to write my book, you immediately got the ball rolling. You have truly been a huge part of this journey, and I am so grateful to have you both on my team.

A big thanks to David, my book agent, who was leading this ship—we did it!

My editor, Meaghan, you truly brought this book to life. Thank you for your insight, expertise, and determination in ensuring my story gets told my way.

Thank you to Harper Horizon, who took a chance on me. After taking meetings from several publishers, we knew instantly that I had found the right home for my book. I am forever grateful you believed in my story from day one.

To my manager, Rana, you came on board and brought this project home. Thank you for letting me confide in you and for listening to all of my thoughts and ideas.

Thank you to my wonderful PR team, who has worked so hard to make this book a success. Heather, you rock!

I have to show love to my best friend, Jake. Your support for everything I do means the world to me, and there is no one else I trusted more to keep this book a secret for so long.

To my amazing family, there is no me without you guys. To Will, thank you for always pushing me to meet my goals. To my older brother, EJ, thanks for always cheering me on. To my wonderful dad, I am always overwhelmed by your love and guidance. Thank you for reminding me that I can do anything I set my mind to. Last but far from least, the biggest thank-you to my mom. This book is as much yours as it is mine. Our stories are intertwined and connected. Thank you for watching episodes with me, jogging my memory on certain events, and being there for me every step of the way. You are my world, and I am honored to be your daughter. I love you all so much.

For the people I didn't name but who have been here along the way, I appreciate your love and support, and it doesn't go unnoticed.

And to my fans and the people who have followed my life for years, I can't thank you enough for the support. You all are the reason I get to finally share my story, because I know you guys truly care about what I have to say.

Notes

Chapter 4: Tales from the Dressing Room

1. *Dance Moms*, season 2, episode 22, "Guess Who's Back?" aired July 24, 2012, on Lifetime, 20:50, https://play.mylifetime.com/shows/dance-moms/season-2/episode-22.
2. *Dance Moms*, season 6, episode 24, "Nia & Kendall Face Off," aired September 13, 2016, on Lifetime, https://play.mylifetime.com/shows/dance-moms/season-6/episode-24.

Chapter 5: At the Bottom

1. *Dance Moms*, season 4, episode 27, "The Understudies," aired September 9, 2014, on Lifetime, 31:28, https://play.mylifetime.com/shows/dance-moms/season-4/episode-27.

Chapter 6: Controversy and Conflict

1. *Dance Moms*, season 2, episode 10, "Miami Heat Wave," aired March 13, 2012, on Lifetime, 10:04, https://play.mylifetime.com/shows/dance-moms/season-2/episode-10.
2. Abby Lee Miller, *Everything I Learned About Life, I Learned in Dance Class* (William Morrow, 2014), 53.
3. "Miami Heat Wave," Dance Moms Wiki, accessed May 23, 2025, https://dancemoms.fandom.com/wiki/Miami_Heat_Wave.

Chapter 7: A New Passion

1. Miranda Siwak, "JoJo Siwa Through the Years: From 'Dance Moms' to Nickelodeon and Beyond," *Us Weekly*, September 14, 2022, https://www.usmagazine.com/entertainment/pictures/jojo-siwa-through-the-years-from-dance-moms-to-nickelodeon/.
2. Bailey Richards, "JoJo Siwa Reveals the Piece of Advice Her Mom Gave Her When She Was the 'Most Hated' *Dance Moms* Cast Member," *People*, September 24, 2024, https://people.com/jojo-siwa-reveals-moms-advice-most-hated-dance-moms-cast-member-8717800.
3. *Dance Moms*, season 5, episode 5, "Hello Hollywood, Goodbye Abby," aired February 10, 2015, on Lifetime, 20:18, https://play.mylifetime.com/shows/dance-moms/season-5/episode-5.

Chapter 10: Token Black Dancer

1. *Dance Moms*, season 1, episode 7, "She's a Fighter," aired August 24, 2011, on Lifetime, 16:55, https://play.mylifetime.com/shows/dance-moms/season-1/episode-7.
2. *Dance Moms*, "She's a Fighter," 17:42.
3. "Dance Moms: Bonus: Debbie Allen Drops By (Season 6, Episode 31)," featuring Debbie Allen and Abby Lee Miller, YouTube, posted by Lifetime, November 3, 2016, https://www.youtube.com/watch?v=i85yEzic6m0.
4. Jill Vertes (@vyxlrc), reply to Christi Lukasiak, Instagram, February 24, 2025, https://www.instagram.com/reel/DGdd18Mziar/?igsh=MWZwMnNueHAxZW5uNw==.
5. *Dance Moms*, season 1, episode 8, "Love on the Dance Floor," aired August 31, 2011, on Lifetime, https://play.mylifetime.com/shows/dance-moms/season-1/episode-8.

Chapter 11: Mothers and Daughters

1. "Dance Moms: Pity Party (Season 2, Episode 5)," featuring Jill Vertes and Melissa Gisoni, YouTube, posted by Lifetime, February 8, 2012, https://www.youtube.com/watch?v=EZDOdBM0Z0c&t=25s&ab_channel=Lifetime.
2. *Dance Moms*, season 2, episode 5, "Brooke's Back," aired February 7,

2012, on Lifetime, 24:23, https://play.mylifetime.com/shows/dance-moms/season-2/episode-5.

Chapter 12: Old Patterns, New Opportunities

1. "Debbie Allen," The Kennedy Center, accessed January 22, 2025, https://www.kennedy-center.org/artists/a/aa-an/debbie-allen/.

Chapter 13: Saying Goodbye

1. *Dance Moms*, season 7, episode 17, "Out with Abby, in with Chloe," aired August 15, 2017, on Lifetime, 6:30, https://play.mylifetime.com/shows/dance-moms/season-7/episode-17.

Chapter 14: Dancing for Myself

1. Melinda Smith and Lawrence Robinson, "Narcissistic Personality Disorder (NPD)," HelpGuide.org, last updated May 5, 2025, https://www.helpguide.org/mental-health/personality-disorders/narcissistic-personality-disorder.

Chapter 15: Life After *Dance Moms*

1. "First-Year Profile—Fall 2023," UCLA Undergraduate Admission, accessed March 21, 2025, https://admission.ucla.edu/apply/first-year/first-year-profile/2023.

Chapter 16: College Years

1. "Our Gun Violence Prevention Initiative," Ad Council, accessed February 24, 2025, https://www.adcouncil.org/.

Chapter 17: Star in Your Own Life

1. Palmer Haasch, "'Stranger Things' Star Caleb McLaughlin Says That Racism in the Fandom 'Took a Toll' on Him as a Child," *Business Insider*, September 27, 2022, https://www.businessinsider.com/stranger-things-caleb-mclaughlin-racism-fandom-2022–9.
2. Abby Lee Miller (@therealabbylee), Instagram, June 4, 2020, https://www.instagram.com/p/CBB25Lwgg4c/?utm_source=ig_embed&ig_rid=3c50648e-c4c5–40a5-adff-2ea3931c12a7.

About the Author

NIA SIOUX is a dancer, singer, and actress who has performed on the small screen and in live performances, proving to be one of today's most popular triple threats. Known for her breakout role as an original cast member in Lifetime's hit series *Dance Moms*, Nia has since starred as a series regular on *The Bold and the Beautiful*. She has appeared in several movies, including *Imperfect High*, and two of her own digital series, one of which she served as an executive producer for. She was featured in *Variety*'s Power of Young Hollywood 2023 list. A graduate of UCLA with a degree in American Literature and Culture, Nia continues to use her social media platforms to positively impact the lives of others. She highlights the accomplishments of inspiring others who have achieved extraordinary things in her Role Model Monday series. Nia is especially committed to encouraging voting, promoting body positivity, and strengthening social justice.